My Summer With Julia

Also by Sarah Woodhouse

Other Lives
Meeting Lily
Enchanted Ground
The Peacock's Feather
The Native Air
The Daughter of the Sea
The Indian Widow
A Season of Mists

My Summer with Julia

Sarah Woodhouse

THOMAS DUNNE BOOKS
ST. MARTIN'S PRESS ✹ NEW YORK

THOMAS DUNNE BOOKS.
An imprint of St. Martin's Press.

MY SUMMER WITH JULIA. Copyright © 2000 by Sarah Woodhouse. All rights reserved. Printed in the United States of America. No part of this book may be used or reproduced in any manner whatsoever without written permission except in the case of brief quotations embodied in critical articles or reviews. For information, address St. Martin's Press, 175 Fifth Avenue, New York, N.Y. 10010.

www.stmartins.com

ISBN 0-312-26622-7

First published in Great Britain by Inner Circle, an imprint of Judy Piatkus (Publishers) Ltd

First U.S. Edition: December 2000

10 9 8 7 6 5 4 3 2 1

For A, J, and Little A

Chapter One

When the letter comes I am painting. The studio is full of light and Pergolesi and the door is locked. I hear the footsteps, the snap of the letterbox, the slap of paper on the tiles. I keep painting. No interruptions while I'm working, please. One of the rules. There have never been many rules but that is the most important. Sam and Gina used to warn other children who came to play: 'Don't make a noise by the studio door,' they'd say, and then I'd hear them tiptoeing by, stifling giggles.

I paint on. In a corner of my mind's eye I see the post on the hall floor, bills probably, a note from Marion – will she or won't she be in Vermont for Easter – and then the usual fevered scrawl from Wim, much underlined: where is the damn picture Annie you promised ring me Lisbon if not Geneva if not Amsterdam. The rest will be oddments, something from Gina's school perhaps, a church bazaar, charities. My brush hesitates for a fraction of a second. Paint on, Annie. Get it over. If you stop this face will defeat you. It's already nine-tenths a lie. Truth has been cobbled into an illusion. The eyes are beautiful and calm, not darting suspiciously as I saw them, and where are the lines of discontent about the mouth? I have painted not what I saw, then, but what I know the sitter wants to see and is prepared to pay for. Is that art? Of a kind. Not my kind. Don't worry about it, David would say, just remember artists must eat like everyone else.

When I lay down the brush the sensation is vertigo. I take time cleaning up while my breathing steadies. I hang my overall tidily, turn off the music. I avoid looking at the easel. In a while I unlock the door and go down the passage to the hall and pick up the post. Nothing from Wim but yes, Marion's elegant spiky hand. 'My mother writes nonsense but she writes it beautifully,' David always says. And it's to be Vermont after all, letting me off the hook. Every year she spends Easter with either David or Tom, though in my opinion (your opinion always seems so sour, Annie dear) she has never cared for either of her sons and would rather stay in London and play bridge. This year it was our turn, but recently Tom acquired a new wife and several stepchildren and a house in the country. Marion, who has been called on expensively in the past when he nose-dived into trouble, is naturally curious. So it will be Vermont and unsuspecting Suzie, not Halingford and dutiful but disagreeable Annie. As I read it occurs to me I have been dutiful but tremendously disagreeable for twenty years, never once Marion's idea of a daughter-in-law, too badly dressed, too likely to reek of turps, too careless of her cherished conventions. We have agreed to disagree, that is about all you can say for our relationship.

I potter about making coffee. There is one more letter. It lies on the table where I have laid it aside, stiff, old-fashioned, a French stamp, bold black ink. Toulouse. I know no one in Toulouse. It is addressed to Mme Annie Somerville, Orchard House, Holybridge Street, Halingford. March sunshine falls across the pages as I open them, smooth them out. It smacks of serious intent, this thick paper, this sooty script. It might be a commission, the offer of an exhibition, who knows?

It is a letter about Julia.

I am not expecting the name. At first I read it as a child would, syllable by syllable, baffled: Ju-li-a, Julia. Who is Julia? Rather, who was Julia? Julia was long ago, oh so long ago, my best friend when I was eight, nine, ten, my best friend until I was fourteen and then suddenly not so best, slipping away, growing up, that summer of the chestnut trees, the *bassin*, the wild boar.

The letter tells me Julia is dead 'as of course you know' – but I don't, I didn't – that she left instructions in her will about certain things, certain objects, possessions which are to be mine. There is a box, *un coffret*, containing these ... things. It is all mysterious. It is like the beginning of a fairy tale, a ghost story. Oh Ju, what silliness now? What did you ever have that I coveted? Besides, you were never one for presents. You never cared for them yourself nor understood that others might.

I sit at the table holding my coffee and the letter. My hand shakes a little. The box, I am told, is at Julia's house in the Cevennes, the house at the well of the Holy Virgin. St Vierge. *That* house. She owned, she lived in – went back deliberately to live in presumably – that house. Why, Julia, why? But Julia won't answer, she's dead at forty-five of something unspecified. Forty-five. No age at all. My age, of course. No, Mme Chartier, how could I know? Who would have told me? The Julia I remember is fourteen for ever, a pale immobile face in the gloom of a French parlour with the blinds drawn. I don't think I have spoken her name in thirty years. There is a shadow sometimes and it moves a little, a very little, and I do know who it is

3

but it remains so faint and distant I can ignore it. And I do.

Mme Chartier is called Monique and she was Julia's mother-in-law, her *belle-mère*. She lives in Toulouse. She says, politely but firmly, that if I want this box I must fetch it. Although small it is heavy, an antique. It would be a trouble to send, do I understand? Yes, I understand. Besides, the lawyer is a scrupulous man, would be happier face to face with this Annie Somerville, would like the usual assurances, perhaps identification. Is there a suspicion in all this that Julia is willing away the family jewels? Haven't they looked inside then? If no one else, the lawyer has the key to the *coffret* and has surely used it. Or the widower? What of him?

Well?

I put the letter back in its envelope. I make more coffee. I try not to think of Julia, Julia at St Vierge, Julia at Charleshall. There was a mulberry, the cool deep water in the *bassin*, the boys made a tree house ... Charleshall, smell of wet dogs, the taste of Dukie's porridge, invigorating bursts of squabbling with the cousins in the dank shrubbery, Julia on the rocking horse.

Come on, Annie, you're wasting time. Better get up, get on with life. All that was in the past and in another place. You've forgotten it.

You've forgotten it, Annie.

I go back to the easel. Now my arms ache lifting the brush though I only have to lift it to write my signature. Reaching for turps, the rag, I find I can't see suddenly, my eyes are full of tears.

'How did it go?' asks Sam. He is home for lunch to humour his old mother. And because he understands

4

my loathing for the picture he wants to see it finished. He doesn't calculate as his father does, each brush stroke a bottle of Rioja, a month's electricity, something towards renting the house in Corsica. He comprehends artistic tensions. Now and again these days he warns me against taking a commission. And I do refuse a few, those bland self-satisfied lumps of faces giving nothing away. I could refuse more but then ... If I were famous, I say to Sam, if, if.

Sam is nineteen, 'doing' architecture at one of the swankier universities, though what he actually does I can't imagine. He tells me I'm crawling about in the undergrowth of prejudice when I fail to appreciate his great blocks of concrete and glass. But it's people like me, I tell him, who shop in them, eat in them, do research in them, sometimes hang paintings in them. I don't want my son responsible for any more of them.

'How did it go?' he asks.

'Finished, thank God.'

'Good.' He is busy making ham and salad sandwiches, plastering in the mayonnaise. He eats the house bare every time he comes in.

'I had the strangest letter this morning.' I find myself breathing quietly, spacing the words. 'About someone I knew when I was a child.'

His blue eyes darken. He doesn't want to hear about when I was a child. A grey world then, unimaginable really, cheese pie for school lunch, for heaven's sake, and short socks till you were fifteen and cinema seats for one and nine.

'Oh yes?' he says, chewing.

'I haven't heard of her in thirty years. Now this.' I'm rubbing it in, which mothers shouldn't do. Reminiscence bores the young. 'She's dead. She's left me a box of ... ' Of what?

'Of what?'

5

'*Objets*.'

Sam is confused. His newly grown-up brow knits, eyebrows careering together. He puts his sandwich down and leans on it because filling keeps falling out.

'So what are *objets*?'

'Don't know. Could be anything, books, letters, a tiara. No, probably not a tiara. That's what I mean by strange. And the people who wrote are anxious about something, about me or this box or maybe about both.'

I give him the letter. He reads it propped against the teapot, his hands being full of sandwich. He frowns and scowls and asks what some of the verbs are, then says, 'Gina'll love this. Sort of Agatha Christie. She's the romantic in this family.'

'Is it romantic?' But he's right, Gina will love it, the suddenness of it, the mystery. My Georgina. A moment ago a fat baby in knickers causing an international incident on the beach at Deauville, hitting a small German boy over the head with her spade and explaining this action in shrieks of English to the intervening French mamas and papas. Georgina. I never liked the name. When she was born I was muddled and exhausted so David chose it. He felt it had old-fashioned charm. As soon as I returned to life I shortened it to Gina.

'So? What are you going to do?' demands Sam.

'About Julia's *objets*? Probably nothing.'

'But aren't you going? I would. Like lightning.'

'All that way?'

He looks at me, head on one side. Pity the old, says his expression. 'It's the nineteen-nineties, Ma dear. You don't have to go on foot or by donkey. Besides,' wiping away mayonnaise from his upper lip, 'you should ring them in ... where was it? Toulouse. Ring them in Toulouse, get facts.'

I watch his hands, large, knuckly, appealing. His

6

father's hands. I look down at my own, paint-stained, wrinkled. Forty-five. Once I could not have imagined forty-five, it had seemed infinitely far off like a view of distant mountains from the plain.

'So when did you last see this Julia?' asks Sam.

'About ... Perhaps '66.' My voice is airy, my so-innocent voice. 'Perhaps '67.'

'And you didn't keep in touch at all?'

'No.'

'Then it *is* strange.' He cocks his head again, waiting for elucidation. 'I mean, why should she leave you anything at all after so long?'

'You never knew with Julia. She sometimes did the unexpected, caught you out.'

Smell of box hedges at Charleshall, feet running on the gravel paths ... I ran about whole afternoons, calling her name, growing exasperated. And of course she wasn't hiding, she'd gone in, was sitting eating biscuits in the kitchen with Dukie. I hate her, I hate her. Juliaaa ...

'Come and look at the face.' I lead Sam to the studio and stand him in front of the easel and watch while he arranges a puckered, noncommittal expression. He makes a great effort. He wants to be kind.

'Well, it's all right,' he concedes at last. 'She'll like it anyway,' this being most of the point. All of it, David would say. 'But you ought to go out and get some sun. Spring's arrived.' He nods towards the garden, takes my elbow like a father. I peer out but see little, being short-sighted: hummocky grass, over-grown shrubs, something dark which must be the summerhouse down by the river.

'It needs rethatching,' says Sam, looking in the same direction.

'Hardly worth it. The walls are rotten.' I love this little folly built of flint and rustic poles and Norfolk

7

reed. There was a time, when I first began to get good prices for pictures, when I planned a larger and more useful hideaway, big enough for a table and chairs, for books, and possibly with opening windows, a proper door. In Belgium once I saw, hanging out over a canal, a perfect Gothic garden house, red brick, white paint, charmingly reflected in the water beneath. 'That's what I'd like,' I told David, who looked dubious then and ever afterwards when it was mentioned. Sometimes I would take a tape measure, pace out the riverbank, draw and plot, but nothing else was ever done, the lines on the paper remained lines on paper. Instead I bought lots of expensive paint and expensive brushes and a new apron, tough as ships' canvas, that will do me as a shroud if necessary.

'You need sunshine,' says Sam, propelling me relentlessly outside. And outside I can see all the gardening I haven't done. There are weeds between the bricks of the paths, weeds in the tubs and pots. Keen green fingers would be out here every morning, busying away. But March is a deceptive month in this part of the world, one moment like this, the next withered by Russian winds. We learn not to toss off our woolly hats till May.

Arm in arm we walk down to the river, a small river, slow and green. Swans nested on the far bank last year and objected every time Gina tried to row the old pram dinghy, hissing and lifting their wings menacingly. Just downstream is one of the town bridges, Holybridge, plain, well-engineered stone, 1780. One crosses into a small pleasant country town, rather old-fashioned. And no harm in that, Sam says, because he likes swans and Georgian bridges and our narrow unpretentious house with its Dutch gables. Inside though he lusts after excitement, after bright lights, the sophistication of cities, the power of raising thirty prize-winning storeys, of being mentioned in the same breath as van der Rohe. He talks of working in London 'to get started' as he puts it. Or Paris, but his French is atrocious. Why not Berlin? His German is passable. But he is unsure about Berlin, he thinks of it as cold and grey, a name in history books. Of course he means to come back one day and do what he can for Halingford, do better anyway than the unsympathetic infills, the chicken-house estates, the heart-sinking supermarket pastiche.

'Go on. Tell me about Julia,' he says as we walk under the willow. Beyond the reeds on the far bank, beyond the swans' winter-ruined nest, are the grazing marshes, acre upon acre. Any day now they will turn out the cattle and we will say 'Look, almost summer' and the next thing will be sleet stripping the pear blossom and everyone back in overcoats and fur boots.

'Julia?' I don't want to talk about Julia.

'Yes, Julia. Why be so cagey?'

'I'm not. There's almost nothing to tell. She came to my school when she was eight. We were friends for a few years. Then there was some kind of drama and she left, never came back. I didn't see her again. The family moved away. I think she married a banker. My mother might have told me or we saw it in the paper. I don't think he was French so this Chartier must have been number two, or three ... who knows? The funny thing is—' I stare down into the water but I see a farmhouse in France, the stony yard, a wall, a blue door being opened by a thin woman in an apron. Arlette. The door is distinctly blue and the woman is obviously Arlette. 'The funny thing is that the house where she lives – lived – is the house where we spent our last holiday together. Her mother used to rent it for a month in the summer. Why there?'

'Why not?'

9

'Because ... Oh, I don't know. I thought she hated the place.' Besides, that house was the scene of ... Of what? I have made a point of forgetting of what for thirty years.

We turn to go in. In spite of the sun the wind is chilly, whips over the marshes. The grass underfoot is too long, much troubled by moles. 'Why can't we have a lawn like everyone else?' I ask David every year, and every year he cuts it and rolls it and feeds it and it looks the same: rough tussocks, mole heaps.

St Vierge. No, I don't really want to think of St Vierge. But the English March wind has a herby, resiny smell; young Annie climbs stiffly out of the car, looking about, sniffing up that southern fragrance tempered by that faint chill of the mountains. Up here, even in summer, nights can be cold. Irresolute young Annie, watching Judith hurrying towards the door, the door opening. Blue door. Arlette. Where is this place? An ancient Cevenole farmhouse built into a hill and with a view of hills. Going inside, a feeling of strangeness, the walls so thick, the beams massive and low. Later, the bed seemed hard, the shadows terrifying. There was no electricity then, just a candle to light us up and leave us in the dark. 'You're silly,' says Julia from across the room in the other bed. 'I know you're crying. Cry-baby.'

In twenty-four hours, less, the strangeness wears away. I love this place, the stone passages, the ashy hearths, the weedy stone terrace, the garden dropping away into the valley. A little further up the track above was the holy well itself, deep and green between boulders. 'It's just an old spring,' says Julia, this new disagreeable Julia. 'And the house is horrible. Primitive. I hate it.' Of course, she has been before, last year and the one before that. I try to remember what she has told me about it, but she has never told me anything. Does she really hate it? Why? I have never seen her so miserable, unreasonable, absent. She always withdraws when she is unhappy, inside herself, up a tree, onto the rocking horse.

Are we all happy except Julia?

'You're not listening, are you?' says Sam. 'Oh, never mind. But did you like her? She must have liked you to have left you something in her will.'

'Perhaps it's the booby prize.' Careful Annie, trying to be light-hearted. Did I like her? She was difficult to like, prickly, secretive, lonely. Well, of course lonely. Something set her apart. Whether it was something imagined or not, still she was apart. Her brothers did not seem brothers to her, her parents only vaguely connected to her, faces across the table at meals. And what was I? I was little and stubborn and solid and sported a ginger pigtail. Carroty Annie they called me at school. Neither Julia nor I were popular girls, joiners-in, team members. We both had family problems, mine obvious and straightforward for my father had been killed in an accident when I was five; Julia's more subtle and confusing; she felt herself unwanted. We gravitated together not to outsmart the bullies but simply because we understood why not to be curious. We asked no questions, did not probe tender spots. We knew how tender such spots can be. I never asked about Charleshall, the car that brought her to school, driven by a gardener, her parents or those younger brothers who troubled her so deeply. She never mentioned my father, the boat, the body washed up long after, my mother's struggle to live by giving music lessons and letting rooms to eccentric lodgers.

'So why didn't you keep in touch?' demands Sam, thirty years on.

'Oh, you know. Time passes. Things get put off, letters don't get written.'

11

He looks at me. Keen eyes, my Sam, keen nose for lies, evasions.

'You're not telling the whole truth,' he says.

Trust a son to find his mother out.

Chapter Two

I feel myself angry, miserable, defensive. I am not going to France.

'I don't know what's got into you,' David says as if talking to a child. But then he thinks I'm behaving like a child. 'Why such a fuss?'

'I'm not making any fuss. You are.'

'But you've finished the picture, haven't you? And you don't need to start the piano child straight away. Why not have a few days off? I'm in New York next week, Sam's off somewhere and there's Greta to have Gina. Why not fly down, hire a car and do a bit of painting while you're there?' He thinks he is being helpful, reasonable. Years ago, when we were struggling, I would have been enchanted by this kind of suggestion. Impossible then, of course – no money ever, two toddlers – but enchanting to think about. And now it was possible it held no special attraction, was even ridiculous.

'How ridiculous,' I hear myself say. 'All that way just for an old box. For a joke.'

'Is it a joke? Well, you should know. She was your friend.' He is peeved, his crumpled face crumples some more. A big shambling man, quite a lot of hair still, certainly a great many lines: character, experience, age. Age, he would say grimly if you asked. He is afraid of growing old. Gina calls him the Bear. They have that close relationship I know nothing about, hardly remembering my own father. They tease each other, they hang over her homework like lovers, separately and in secret they grumble affectionately about each other's foibles. I know that when David is an old man his face will still light up when Gina steps into a room.

'Mum doesn't want to go,' puts in Sam. He looks David in the eye.

'But I want to know why,' says David.

'I wouldn't mind going to Aunt Greta,' Gina chirps in case they've forgotten she is there.

'It's out of the question,' I tell her. And I hear my own mother's voice suddenly, saying the same thing. Out of the question, you haven't any clothes, enough clothes, four weeks in France ... Whatever next? But she laughed as she said it. 'Do you want to go? Then of course you must.' She never grudged me to them, these wealthy and rather careless people. There had been weekends in London, weeks in Cornwall and the Cairngorms, holiday after holiday at Charleshall. She had to work and there was Tottie to worry over and she had never been able to or never wanted to provide us with a father or any kind of substitute. Sometimes, perhaps often, she must have been lonely. But she thought friends were precious and Julia was my friend, how could she keep us apart? She never interfered, only subtly rearranged dates or means of transport on the phone to Julia's mother. I sensed she felt sorry for Julia's mother, which puzzled me. Judith was elegant, young-looking – she must only have been in her early thirties – rather absent-minded. I was silly enough to think my mother felt, and felt she looked, the poor widow, except for that one time at Charleshall, at the piano. But then, though children sniff atmospheres

14

infallibly, they rarely know what has caused them.

Part of being grown up is knowing which memories to leave undisturbed. Or, as Julia's grandmother said to me on that strange journey home from France, it doesn't do to dwell on the past. And how right she was. Already that damn letter has had an effect. I don't know about Julia's box, this is my box, marked Keep Locked, and the lid is up, Julia is out, Judith, Arlette, the grandmother ... Soon will come the Major, Monsieur Blanchard, Alain.

'Look, I don't want to talk about it. I'm not going,' I say. I sound a cross middle-aged female. I get up from the breakfast table where we are all glaring at each other, and go for my painting apron. If in doubt, Annie, get businesslike.

'Bye,' says Gina, putting her head round the studio door.

'Have you lunch money?'

'I'll ask Daddy.'

David comes, gives me a peck. 'What's all this about lunch money?' He is still disgruntled. His office is only up the road but this morning, to work off any bad temper, he will go the long way by the river, crossing at the sluice. He will probably get his polished shoes muddy. His partner, Will, a fastidious young man, would never dream of coming to work in muddy shoes. A nice boy for all that, the very new father of a daughter who cries continuously or so I'm told. A few weeks of this and his priorities will rearrange themselves, the knot of his tie will be less than perfect, he will forget his appointment for a haircut, he will show himself as imperfect and harassed and human as the rest of us.

'You look a wreck,' says David comfortingly as he departs. 'Is there something you haven't told me?'

'About what?'

15

He bangs the front door to show what he thinks of artists and wives.

I can't paint. I take a long time washing out all the brushes, tidying up, and then ring the piano child's mother and fix an appointment. Something achieved, however small, eh Annie? Continuing in this dutiful vein I write a letter to Marion giving her all the news, which is nothing out of the ordinary and in which she has no interest whatsoever. She would prefer to be telephoned for then some excuse can always be found for ringing off, the hairdresser or one of her little lunch parties. Our twenty-year acquaintance means nothing, leaves us still strangers, uneasy at prolonged contact. I imagine her confiding to her chiropodist that her daughters-in-law have both been disappointments, the one unfaithful, the other temperamentally uncertain and with hair like a stork's nest.

I seal the letter, put on a stamp and feel the momentary triumph of petty virtue. But poor Marion, forced to read – perhaps she won't, perhaps she throws these away unread – about her granddaughter's school play, Sam's Bauhausian ambitions. She never wanted marriage or a family, these were simply a convention she followed because nothing else occurred to her. She never wanted a career either. She is happy being decorative, making sure she never looks her age, gossiping with her gossipy friends, playing cards. She is profoundly sensible, knows to a penny the value of every piece of jewellery she possesses. She should have been a king's mistress, an object of occasional pleasure, no bother to anyone. It would not occur to her to interfere in matters of state, for instance. Do I make her sound frivolous or stony-hearted? She is neither of those. She has rescued Tom many times, beginning when he was at school. If you asked she would say it was a mother's obligation, though her concept of motherhood is vague, she would rather not be one. 'She is really rather amazing,' David says, though what he means by the word is debatable, and when she comes to stay he finds her infuriating, as unapproachable as she was when he was a small boy, as sophisticated, as selfish.

I go outside. Is life easier if you are a Marion? I don't know what I mean by easier. I don't really know what gives her pleasure, the kind of pleasure the children, painting, the river, gives me. Today there is a cold wind ruffling the water and I surprise a heron on the far bank who flaps away over the marshes. Someone told me yesterday that the swans are nesting by the millpond this year. Very sensible. It is quieter there, no danger from the cattle and plenty of room for parental squabbles, all that thrashing about with extended necks and frantic wings. 'They're dangerous,' Gina cried more than once, turning circles in the leaky old boat, flailing her oars. And they were, being crotchety and always on the defence. As a parent I know how they felt.

I sit in the summerhouse. The rustic bench, big enough for two, is abrasive, uncomfortable. The water slips by. Birds twitter in the willow. I can't see them, the willow is a blur. And that was another thing, another thing that made me an ugly duckling: glasses. At twelve I had to wear glasses to see the blackboard. Instead of being pretty and unblemished I was small, clumsy and wore glasses. Some stray ancestor had made sure I turned out a surprise. My mother was a woman of wide cheekbones, huge appealing eyes, fair, heavy hair. In photographs my father looks tall and conventionally handsome. 'But you were a sweet baby,' was what I was told consolingly.

Tottie was not a sweet baby. She screamed all day

and most of the night. I would have been tempted to chuck her from a window. Perhaps my mother was. Being a mother is a series of such agonised self-restraints: one could kill them or kill for them every day. Tottie might have been a pretty baby but all we saw of her was a furious red complexion, an open mouth. She went back and forth to the doctor but medical science was baffled. In reality they probably thought my mother hysterical. Women who have babies two months after being widowed may very well behave oddly. Or perhaps Tottie's yelling was for the father she would never know and who would never know her. I don't remember why we called her Tottie. Her real name was Margaret and when she grew up a bit she declared she wanted to be known as Greta. 'And she always has her own way,' said my mother.

I stare across at the marshes. Soon the cattle will be there, swishing at flies, chewing the cud, grooming each other lazily. In summer we live in an Aelbert Cuyp. The river will fall a little and small birds will flit in and out of the reeds. Sam might paint the boat and we can picnic downriver the way we used to when he was small, armed with fishing lines and jam jars and tomato sandwiches. Passing under the bridge he always hooted with fright, closing his eyes so as not to see the dripping stone, the green slime.

I can't sit all morning looking at grass and water. I should be working. I should be ... What? Ringing Mme Chartier, asking what about these *objets*? Surely she knows what they are? I go in, do unnecessary jobs in the kitchen, put some washing in the machine. Then I stand over the phone for several minutes before dialling, like a little girl poised on the edge of a swimming pool. Being grown up means not being pushed in, I had thought, longing for the day. That was when I had met Julia properly, until then a shadowy figure, a

18

new girl who kept always to herself. 'Go and pick on someone else,' she said calmly to my tormentor, and put herself between us, meaning business. A new girl, daring to do this.

Julia.

I pick up the receiver. I have weathered, stained, ageing hands. Not the small girl hands that held Julia's in gratitude, both of us toppling, laughing, into the water. I can't imagine why I'm ringing this number. If no one answers I shan't try again. No, no one there. They are out at the market, the *boulangerie*. Then he answers, a gruff cultured French voice. I can see him standing there, polished shoes, good trousers, check shirt, sweater, an English country look, old-fashioned. And old-fashioned manners. He is very formal.

I explain myself. My French is decent but rusty. Words escape me. I have to use simple expressions. *La plume de ma tante*. But the accent passes, you can tell I was taught French by a Frenchwoman.

'My wife is out,' he says. 'These things are not easy to discuss on the telephone. I understood Julia,' and he pronounces it Shjoolia, a kindly noise, 'has left you this box. It is ready for you. At St Vierge. Everything,' and he is emphatic, 'is being done properly.'

Have I suggested it is not? But what did she write in her will? '... And the mahogany box to my old friend Annie Somerville ...' Oh, come on. Absurd. After all these years? And as I stand, phone in hand, I see the cat pause in the middle of the kitchen floor, dabbing a paw at one ear as if in two minds whether to wash. Who would take care of him if I died? David would forget for certain.

'Is there a time I could speak to Madame? This evening?' I press.

'We naturally assumed you would visit us,' he says.

19

He is speaking slowly for my benefit, ignorant Englishwoman muddling her tenses. Or is he giving himself time? He is nervous. He doesn't want anything to do with all this. What did he say? 'I understood Julia has left you this box ...' As if he wasn't sure, really knew nothing much about it. Of course he knows. Of course they listened to the will and then asked who is this Annie Somerville, never heard of her, and why that box, and what's in it? Anyone know what's in it?

'I don't know if I can come.'

'But surely ... Well, yes, my wife will be here this afternoon. We are eating out. Perhaps if you could call before six.'

There is some noise in the background, voices, a distant klaxon. An ordinary French morning. Toulouse. But I might be talking to another planet. Thank you, I say. Goodbye. Au revoir. We are quite animated over these small pleasantries. They cost nothing and come easily. It is only when I return to the studio I find I am shaking, my hands are shaking, I have to sit and wait, breathing deeply, before I can carry on. Putting on my apron, picking up a brush – these actions, normally so soothing, make me tense again. I put up the fresh canvas I prepared for the piano child, that mite who is the most precious object in her father's life and who will pay for it. In this child, seated at her piano, I have seen my mother's ardent joy and passionate involvement. I've also seen the inward shrinking of the hard-driven, the singled-out. Music means a great deal to me but I only listen to it ... My mother could not draw to save her life. *Chacun* whatever. But today the little girl must wait. I'll do her another canvas tomorrow.

Think, Annie. Think. I do, frowning down at the palette. 'You look like a hag before you start,' Sam always says, 'and like an old witch when you've finished.' He should know. He sat in his high chair while I painted, breaking wax crayons and tearing paper. 'Perhaps you should wear your glasses,' he suggests occasionally. Humour old mother, she still thinks she might have some talent. I think, think, reach out ...

The first line. The whole face is already there but this first line marks a boundary, the territory accorded brow and cheek. Now another, another. I work on and on for what seems hours and is exactly an hour and a half which is more than I can usually stand, my arms growing old and weak along with the rest of me. Now I stop, stand back, refuse to look. The sun has moved round, the wind is rattling the glass. I feel tired.

When I glance up there is Julia – almost Julia. She is impatient, angry, haughty. She was often like this, but only for brief moments, the times she felt ignored, overlooked. Did she ever take it out on me? No. I don't remember. No. On the boys, yes. She could be spiteful, horrible to the poor boys. But I was just Annie, was just there, she had asked me to be there. So is this Julia? How do you paint a face from memory? One doesn't remember faces. We say, she was fat, thin, had a big nose. We recapture a shape only for an instant, the sculpture of bone, the way hair falls, and then it's gone and we only think we remember. How do I paint a face I only think I remember?

It is a child's face I paint, but I am no longer the child who once knew it well. I have to peer backwards down a frightening tunnel of years. Thirty years, Annie. More. And can you see that dark silky hair against her cheek, the smile she kept for Dukie, the way she would run, chin up, her arms flung out as if she hoped to take off?

Julia, Julia, are you there?

21

David thinks she is a joke. He can't believe in the thirty years' silence. Being a lawyer he is used to the bizarre, the petty and ridiculous fallings-out of neighbours, the strange domestic habits of married couples. Yet he is surprised I didn't keep in touch, send cards at Christmas, for christenings, illness, anniversaries. He thinks women are good at this sort of thing. Holding the threads, he calls it. 'I suppose you didn't really like her,' he says. This strikes him as a plausible explanation. I let it go. I'm not ready to tell the truth. Do I know the truth? Yes, but I've piled thirty years over it, stamped it well down. This is why Julia's face is a mess, in my mind, on the canvas. Careless, Annie, Wim would say, all this throwing paint about. What are you up to, woman? And he would glance at me, eyebrows raised, wondering.

I perch on the edge of the table among the pots of geraniums. I look out at the garden, a blur of damp heaving bushes, agitated greenery.

I think: surely the dead can do no harm to the living?

My mother declared she would miss me, four weeks was a long time. She spoke cheerfully, but clearly had genuine misgivings. 'Julia never comes here,' she said. 'You do ask her?' 'She won't come,' I told her. 'She never goes anywhere. She says if she leaves Charleshall they'll forget all about her.' I didn't know if my mother would make anything of this. I thought it rather silly. I only repeated it because, however odd, it seemed to be the truth. It was nothing to do with Julia considering herself too grand, our narrow Edwardian house too small, my mother Bohemian, the lodgers eccentric or our food exotic, though all these things had been suggested at school where it was also known Julia never visited me. She never notices these things,

I could have said. They mean nothing to her. But stuck-up Julia, they said, nobody's good enough for her, not even Annie.

What did my mother really think? Who knows? I sometimes suspect she was careful what she packed for me when I took my Hawsley holidays. Julia never had to wear second-hand clothes. In her family only outdoor coats and boots and hats were borrowed, exchanged or handed out indiscriminately. She had few clothes other than schoolwear, all top quality and boringly sensible. We didn't care about such things then, only that we didn't look ridiculous. I don't think I ever told Julia that my winter coats, classic cut and cloth, usually came from my Aunt Faith who had married a Harley Street consultant and shopped accordingly. 'Good clothes never wear out,' said my mother. She made me feel it was a privilege to wear them. But to Julia they would have been just coats, blue or grey or brown, things to put on when it was cold.

I don't paint Julia's clothes. Not yet. She is on the rocking horse, leaning forwards, her head on her arms. She is looking at me. I can't even tell yet how old she is. Twelve? Thirteen? We took turns on the rocking horse for years, a very old horse and much rocked by generations of careless children. 'My thinking place,' Julia said once and then frowned, turning away, because she never usually gave such things away. Yes, that crosspatch look, the go-away-don't-touch-me stare. But in an hour and a half how can I draw a face I haven't seen for God knows how long? It is her and it isn't. And nowhere have I been delicate or sympathetic. There is just a great deal of emotion one way or another, the paint laid on brazenly. Ah well. Early days, Annie.

Yesterday I was looking at portraits by Roger van

der Weyden thinking: these are people I should like to meet. The man liked his subjects, had a sense of humour. He would have a poor opinion of my Julia, this half-formed face. Where is her dignity? he would ask. Was she never happy, thoughtful, brave? Did you care nothing for her? Well, wait a bit, I tell him. Give this artist time. Wait a bit and maybe a truer Julia will appear.

'I'm home,' cries David from beyond the studio door.

'Self-evidently,' I say, emerging.

'You might have thought I was a burglar.'

'When I'm painting I wouldn't notice,' I tell him. I put on the kettle. He rarely comes home before six. He is conscientious, a man of habit. He chose to set up his legal practice in this small town because he has ideals, mostly muddled, about easy access to justice and old ladies unable to use public transport. He draws up a lot of wills and spends a great deal of time explaining Brussels law to small businessmen who fall foul of it. Last year they asked him to open the town fête. 'I think it means they like you,' I told him.

'Sam?' he asks as I put the tea in front of him.

'At the pub.'

'I never had the money to spend all afternoon in a pub,' he says wistfully, looking back. 'Besides, they weren't open in the afternoon in those days.'

We sit opposite each other and I notice I have green paint on my hands as I pick up my cup. Probably in my hair too.

'Have you rung the Chartiers?' he asks in a soft voice. Only asking out of politeness, he means me to understand. He's not curious. God forbid, why should he be curious?

'I got Monsieur,' I tell him. 'Not very forthcoming. Told me to ring again when Madame was at home.'

24

'You should go. Listen, a few days in France ...'

'I'd rather Bermuda.'

'Can't afford Bermuda. Besides, it'll be spring in Toulouse. Real spring. Not like this.' And he nods at the blustery English weather outside.

We drink more tea.

'You don't want to go,' he says.

'I don't know.' Do I even want to talk about it? 'I don't know. It's like opening the door of a room you shut up so long ago you've forgotten what was in it.'

'Spooky?'

'Spooky.'

Later he stands in front of the easel not knowing what to say. He never has any idea what to say about the paint but faces interest him.

'Was she pretty?' The last question I'm expecting.

'Yes ... Perhaps. Dark hair, very straight, grey eyes. Not at all like her mother. Like her grandmother must have been.'

And I hear that firm upper class old voice, feel the bony hand, so immensely, unexpectedly strong. We are in a station buffet, Paris probably. There is bustle and chatter and a great noise of plates and excited foreigners and trains. I am tired and a little confused but I'm still receiving impressions: hubbub, cooking smells, the grip of those grandmother fingers with their flashing rings. 'It doesn't do, Annie,' she is saying. Were there tears in her eyes or am I putting them there thirty years later? 'No, it doesn't do. Shall we have the omelette?'

'Something happened,' says David.

He waits. I don't reply. He moves to admire the geraniums which he never expects to survive, fondling their leaves until he has raised that distinct acrid summery smell. He never minds being patient. It costs little, he always says, and in the end people invariably

25

offer up their secrets. He likes to think of himself as a psychiatrist and a priest as well as a country solicitor.

'Let's go out tonight,' he says. 'We could book a table at The Mill. We haven't been frivolous for God knows how long.'

I know how he wants to be frivolous in the next half hour but pretend ignorance and fiddle about with canvases. Gina is due back from school, Sam from that everlasting pub. I don't want my children to catch me in bed with their father at four in the afternoon. Old-fashioned, you might say.

So I ring Toulouse and Monsieur answers and tells me Madame is lying down, she cannot speak tonight, could I call tomorrow. *Demain*, he says twice, making sure I have understood. They cannot go out, it is a great pity, but there is this headache. Madame is prone to headaches. But tomorrow evening, about eight ... And they are both hoping I can visit, they would be delighted to drive me to collect the box.

But what is in the box?

And here is Gina, crashing in, distraught. 'I've lost my scarf. Some awful boy took it.'

'What boy? Why let him?' demands David who, for all his mildness, has always instructed her to punch the bloke where it hurts and run.

'It happened before I knew,' she says pathetically. Her face is pink. He folds her in his arms as if her life has been threatened. But I know she is upset because the other girls failed to defend her. Friends are supposed to stand by you in a crisis.

'We'll get it back,' I tell her. There will be endless letters to the headmaster, phone calls, delay. Schools these days are strangled by bureaucracy. No more making an example of the boy in front of the class, ruler on knuckles, cane on bottom, hand it back or else.

And Gina says the thief was at least six foot five, built like a heavyweight boxer and mentally unstable, bottom of the whole pack of them in everything but strong-arm tactics. David and I exchange looks.

'Never mind,' says David. 'Your mother's tough too.'

Chapter Three

Wim rings. He is in an airport lounge or the lobby of a hotel. He wants to know why I haven't been in touch, what I'm painting. 'What are you painting, Annie? Something for me?' I imagine him, tall and thin, hunched over the phone trying to hear my reply. My reply is vague, and negative. 'Look ...' says Wim.

He gives me a lecture. I hear it imperfectly over the babble of human activity. Besides, why should I listen?

'Where are you?' I ask.

'Where are *you*, Annie?' He is always swift to turn the tables. 'This is you we are talking about, your life, your career. Your future, Annie.'

Silence. Am I supposed to take this seriously? I do. I do. But laughter bubbles up.

'Up a creek without a paddle,' I tell him.

'What?'

'Where I am.'

'Why must you be so facetious?' admonishes David. 'Wim believes in you.'

He likes Wim because he believes Dutchmen to be sober and uncomplicated. Besides, it was Wim who began to charge the high prices for my portraits so that, for the first time, we could pay off the overdraft.

'He knows I hate sermons. Especially sermons down the phone.'

'You haven't done anything but commissions since that purple thing.'

'That purple thing was Nancy Brewer in a new dress. You know that. You know people always dress oddly for portraits.'

'They seemed to be having a tantrum. She and the dress.'

'You don't like my paintings much, do you? All these years ...'

Now we are going to get silly. It is, after all, the privilege of old married couples to argue pointlessly.

'I think your pictures are amazing,' he says ambiguously.

For want of anything better I throw my breakfast toast at him and get marmalade on his tie.

'It's time you grew up,' he tells me.

Later I paint. I don't paint Julia, I take her off the easel and turn her face to the wall. I start on a landscape entirely for myself, neither a commission nor to sell. It goes badly. In the end I begin to paint over it, wasting a lot of vermilion. Vermilion is how I feel today.

Later still I go out. I go up Holybridge Street, Hill Street and into the market square. It is market day. The sky is iron-grey, then driven white, then sharp pellets of hail strike down. People shiver and take shelter, laughing and calling out. A moment later and the sun is out, there are birds singing in the gardens behind the shops.

This is why we live in this place. Distances are small, shopkeepers friendly, birds sing behind the shops. David's office is in an eighteenth-century town-house with a view of the water meadows. There is a

29

proper weekly market with a fish stall and a cheese stall and local knobby vegetables and wrapping paper and plants and a man who sells only pig meat: bacon, ham, trays of pathetic trotters. The rest of the world scurries to hypermarkets but here we still gossip over herring and rhubarb, green beans and tea towels. On this one day we stop the traffic, stopping to talk in the road.

I wonder, as I pick and pluck up and put down, if Madame Chartier is doing the same in a French square under the limes. There are no limes left in Halingford. There were chestnuts once, you can see them in old photographs. No doubt the council had them removed in the interests of public safety; bureaucracy hangs many a hat on this peg.

Madame Chartier. Julia. Julia with a French mother-in-law, a woman who often gets headaches and has to lie down. An excuse? Possibly. They seem anxious about the box. Were they fond of her, of Julia? I don't even know the name of their son. Where is the son? Are there children?

I'm not running to look for her. I'm not. I'm standing shivering in the cold spring years and years in the future. Juliaaa ...

Back in the house the phone is ringing.

Greta says: 'Well of course I'll have Gina if you're going. You are going?' without any preamble as if we have been discussing this for at least fifteen minutes. David has called her from work then.

'No.'

'Not going? You need a break, Annie. David's right. You've been working hard for months.'

'The last thing I need is you and David organising my life.'

'Oh, come on, Annie ...'

But she doesn't know the story of that summer, my

30

very last summer with Julia. Nothing was ever said. In those days things weren't said, one kept quiet, carried on. What happened to Julia or to Julia's mother was not really our business, we had simply been bystanders. The events had taken place under our noses but we had not been involved, had been innocent, perhaps ingenuous, had never smelt tragedy in the air.

'You're just like Mother,' Greta is saying. 'Just stubborn.'

It has never occurred to me I am in any way like my mother. In a blink of memory I see her with her beautiful hands on the piano keys, her head bent, listening for the revelation in the music. 'I'm second-rate, Annie,' she told me once. But I have never thought so. It was just that her genius had been cut in the bud, had not survived marriage and widowhood and the years of cheap music lessons, the demanding lodgers.

'If I could get away ... ' Greta is still talking. 'I'd love to come with you. Marion could come up and look after Gina, do her bit.'

I think of Marion in the beautifully furnished house David was never allowed to untidy. Gina admires her, I think, but from a distance, as one might admire one of the smaller prettier cats at a zoo, an ocelot, a serval.

'Marion's off to Vermont,' I say.

'Oh well. I couldn't come anyway. Rob's coming home for ten days. He can drive Gina to school, she hates the bus.'

'She doesn't really.' I'm thinking: what lives we lead, coming home to kick off our shoes for ten days, take someone else's child to school, fly off again.

There is this silence. I become aware of it gradually. She wants to ask something but can't marshal the words. Never very subtle, Tottie. If she wanted something when she was little she generally yelled. If she

31

got it and hated it she threw it away or spat it out and then yelled to be consoled.

'Annie ... There's nothing wrong?'

'Why should there be? Only a portrait I'd rather chuck out and start again except I know the next one would be worse.' I know she has no sympathy with any of this. I sometimes feel we communicate with each other down a long tunnel, small figures making jerky, often wrongly interpreted gestures like semaphore.

'Look, Annie ...' she begins again.

I go and clean up the kitchen.

Then I escape to the summerhouse whose roof is temporarily beaded with little hailstones. The wind is icy, the sun blotted out by tremendous cloud. Winter scene. I shiver, sit tenderly on the rustic planks, blow on my gloved fingers. A long way from the Cevennes in July. Then why do I hear us shrieking as we plunge into the deep green of the *bassin*? We are shrieking not because of the cold but because of the snakes; Arlette has told us adders swim there sometimes in the heat of the day.

A punt slides into view propelled by a hunched figure in a raincoat with a sack over its shoulders. Old Harry Moy come to give me advice about the fruit trees. He lives the other side of town, but as the river loops round and he is more at home on water than land, he poles here in his own time. His grandfather's wherry used to tie up on the far side of the bridge in the days when the river was navigable to the sea.

'You need a thicker coat,' he begins, 'do you'll catch a cold.'

He is something between eighty and ninety. His face is scarlet from pushing that long unwieldy punt against the stinging wind. He pats my hand, treating me like a daughter, seven years old and doesn't know any better. To please him I go in and put on a coat of David's, ancient Welsh tweed. It touches the ground on me, the collar scratches my chin. He nods approval. We set off amiably to view the trees.

'Old trees don't stand interfering,' he says. He lays a hand on the trunks like a doctor feeling for the pulse. He knows them of old. 'Leave well alone,' he counsels.

Walking back to his punt I say: 'I might be going to France.'

'I hope you enjoy it.' He last saw France in 1944 and this colours his opinions.

'I don't really mind if I go or not.'

He looks up and down the river. 'Have to get at these banks come summer. If it's got to be done best get it over with. New picture, is it?'

'No. An old friend has died.'

He clicks his tongue. 'I don't hold with funerals,' he says. 'All that solemn stuff. But the cake and beer afterwards, that's all right.'

Julia is already buried, so no cakes and ale at the wake for me. I wonder who went, who wept, who didn't weep. There must have been women there who knew her better than I did, knew the grown Julia, the wife, the Frenchwoman. Did they put her to rest with the Chartiers in some graveyard overburdened with large tombs and fulsome inscriptions?

I go to the studio and prepare a canvas. Large. When I am feeling emotional my paintings are bigger. There is profound satisfaction in wallowing in tides of paint. And this is for the piano child, that pale steely little thing with the tyrannical father.

Julia, where did you go?

I don't want to think about Julia.

I leave everything ready for the picture, then pick the dead leaves off the geraniums, then feed the cat.

33

I try not to think of Julia buried.

At the appointed hour I ring Madame Chartier. She
answers at the second ring as if she is waiting by the
phone. Her voice sounds quavery, older than his. Then
I decide she must be talking through a handkerchief or
has a sore throat.

'It's quite a small box, an old writing slope.
Mahogany.' Acajou, she says. I have to look it up
afterwards.

'Do you know what's in it?'

'But of course no one has looked. It is locked. The
lawyer has the key.'

'But your son, Julia's husband, surely he ...'

'But he is also dead, Madame. Neither of them
survived the accident. I thought you knew this.'

I hear myself apologising. Her voice has grown
firmer, I notice. It takes courage to talk of her son and
this stiffens her, upholds her.

'Please,' she says. 'My brother lives twenty miles
from St Vierge, he would be pleased to put you up
while you meet the lawyer.' She has already planned
everything, so that justice is done, so I might not
disturb their lives more than is necessary. But then,
language is tricky. There are inflections of the voice,
traces of bitterness. There is also scope for imagining
these things.

'If I come, it will be a very quick visit,' I tell her.

'We would be so pleased.' Not sounding pleased.

'Julia ...'

But she is not talking about Julia either.

'Tell me about Julia,' says David in bed, but I turn
over and pretend to be half asleep. I can't pretend to be
properly asleep because I have only just finished my
nightly tussle with Henry James and turned off the light.

'In the morning,' I murmur.

'Annie, in the morning you'll find some other excuse.'

'Oh, shut up.'

He creaks about a little to get comfortable. Probably he would be glad to throttle me. He is a heavy man and I roll into his hollow. We lie in lover-like togetherness, breathing in harmony, childishly cross with each other. Whatever we try – beds that zip together, an extra large bed that nearly brings down the ceiling, separate beds – is a failure. He weighs fifteen stone, I weigh eight. So we are back in our Victorian double bed with the firmest of firm mattresses into which he sinks a good six inches.

'David ...' My eyes are open. 'Why would anyone want to go a thousand miles for an old box?'

'Friendship?'

'But after thirty years.'

He is having none of this.

'You need to sort yourself out,' he says.

I meet Greta two days later. We drive to the sea and lunch at a pub full of birdwatchers. Something interesting must have been reported. They stand about with their pint glasses, animated, laughing and quaffing. They wear expensive binoculars like chains of office. They are all sensibly dressed too, which is more than Greta is who has just come from interviewing her youngest daughter's headmistress, apparently a formidable woman with bright blue contact lenses. 'She wears them to put you off your stroke,' Greta says. 'Why is it one never gets anywhere with teachers?'

'Because they talk to you as if you're a child and so you become one again.'

But there is still something of the child in Greta, something of Tottie, all those violent desires and rejections. She is taller than me and still pretty, fair-haired. Carefully made up, in a smart little grey suit, she looks intelligent and concerned, the model nineties mother.

'This Julia Hawsley,' she says. 'Why haven't I ever heard of her?'

I am not ready to tell anyone about Julia. This is not deliberate evasion, simply that Julia can't be fitted into words nor words fitted round Julia. Not yet.

'It's getting busy,' I say. 'I'd better order.'

The birdwatchers hide me from her. With luck when I return she will want to talk about herself or her children or Rob or the woman with blue contact lenses who is a role model for budding tyrants.

'A ploughman's, the prawns,' I tell the barman. He has a huge round face, looks sweatily perplexed. He has been put out by the bird people, flocking in on a quiet weekday.

A fair woman is leaning on the bar. I see only the back of her head, slim shoulders. Judith. My heart sinks away, I drop the change which the man scoops up again and presses into my palm. Judith. But of course it isn't Judith, Judith was Julia's mother and is dead. I begin on the journey back to the table and it seems endless, obstructed at every turn. Someone's elbow catches me in the face; he is demonstrating a bird's flight. Beer spills. I can't see Greta. I can see Judith though. She is sitting on the steps of the porch at Charleshall and there is a King Charles spaniel beside her, red and white. Lottie. I remember now. The dog was called Lottie. And Judith said, smiling, 'Annie, your hair is so lovely. Like candle flames.' She was the only person who ever praised it. Julia called it foxy. My mother said she didn't know where I'd got it as if I had picked it up off the street. But Judith said it was like candle flames.

'Annie,' says Greta. 'Annie.'

'It's crowded. You can't hear yourself think,' I say tritely.

'Look, where did this Julia live?'

'A house called Charleshall. Near Thetford.'

'I don't remember it.'

'Why should you?'

'What was it like?'

Red brick, sash windows, glasshouses with grapes but no heating in the house but coal fires; Stone-Age plumbing, lots of larders, pantries, a vast wine cellar. Shabby genteel. No one uses that phrase nowadays. After the war there was a lot of shabby genteel, old houses going quietly to ruin, sold up or pulled down. Charleshall was lucky because it belonged to an estate and the people in the big house were new, had made money in armaments or aeroengines or something. They fancied themselves as squires. All the same, plaster was cracked, rugs were threadbare. The Hawsleys had lost their own Charleshall and had come to this one as tenants. A come-down, I heard someone say. Julia's father managed the estate where once he had managed his own. 'And he's not a man to take that philosophically,' said my own mother who had once charmed a wintry smile from him, more than anyone else, I felt, had ever done.

I remember the big rooms at Charleshall full of sunlight. I remember the great vases of flowers Judith loved, and polished floors, blankets thrown over the faded silk upholstery for the dogs. In my mind people pass in and out, into drawing rooms and greenhouses and the soapy leathery linseedy tack room. They wear moleskin and tweed and shiny shoes that creak and a variety of hats depending on their status or the weather. There is no-nonsense carbolic soap to wash your hands and in summer the front door always stands open so that rose petals and sometimes birds drift into the hall. Sheets are white and stiff, the baths deep and ancient. The grey rocking horse on the landing is the size of a real pony. We rock here on rainy days. We never grow too old for this, it is our special place. Perhaps on the rocking horse for which, unlike everything else, Julia is content to wait her turn, she is at her best. Best Julia, content, relaxed, soothed by the motion. She never rocks fast unless I ride with her. Then the floorboards creak horribly and the sparse mane flies up and I feel the frightening surge of her happiness. But she is kinder to this wooden horse than she is to the real pony in the stables. She doesn't care for the pony, he is too strong-willed for her, stronger-willed than she is – he makes her look a fool in front of the Major.

Judith. The Major. He didn't seem like a father, like other girls' fathers, he was too remote. He took the boys out shooting, they had their own small guns. Once he rode by with one in front, one behind him in the saddle. He appeared more at ease with his sons though they were ill at ease with him, burdened with his high expectations. And the grandparents? Judith's father, a mild, sweet-tempered man who took all day to read *The Times*; the Major's mother, always in such perfectly tailored black, smelling faintly of lavender water and moth balls. Then there was Mrs Duke the housekeeper, and a cook, Mrs Salmon, and two girls who came every day from the village. There were gardeners, Prentice in the stables, the rabble of cousins, their parents, their nannies. I remember nannies. And aunts and great-aunts, forthright Edwardians, who told children to wash their faces or eat up their greens. And dogs everywhere, Labradors, pointers, Lottie.

'Annie,' says Greta.

She can't understand why this place means nothing to her. Did she never visit? Who had delivered me, collected me? Judith Hawsley, I tell her, in an elderly station wagon filled with picnic rugs, cartridge bags, dog hairs, dogs. She looked cool and pretty in our front room which Mother had painted a deep blue and hung with the paisley silk curtains from her grandfather's St Petersburg house.

'None of this means anything to me,' says Greta, pained. The food has come and she has started straight away, always eager, always greedy.

'Too wrapped up in yourself. Anyway, you were only nine when I last saw Julia.' I recall a gang of little girls dominated by Greta all week at school and all weekend in our jungly garden. Tottie then, of course, not Greta. And Mother worrying, always worrying. 'I never know what she's up to. She doesn't stop to think of consequences. She doesn't stop to think at all.'

'You had a pigtail,' says Greta.

Pigtail, freckles, glasses. I took the glasses off at Charleshall. I lived happily in a blurred world. There were always smells: pinks, roses, catmint, lemon balm, lavender, apples, baking cakes, carbolic, wet dogs, hot horses, earth, old tweed, cigars, starched linen. I didn't need glasses. I could tell where I was with my eyes closed.

'So what went on that summer in the Cevennes?' Greta is always persistent.

'Just a holiday.'

'But I get the impression you don't want to talk about it. So does David.'

She is chasing the last few prawns round her plate. Over her shoulder I can see some of the birdwatchers earnestly consulting a map. There are no maps to the past, I want to say, no straight paths.

'Julia's mother died in France,' I tell her. 'There

39

was a bit of a drama, played down because of the children. I was sent home with the grandmother.'

'Just the two of you?'

I nod. 'By train. Extraordinary journey.' I don't say in what way it was extraordinary. Besides, she isn't interested in it, she is still trying to link herself to these lost years: where was *she*? What was *she* doing?

'And you never saw Julia again?'

'They took her away from school. The family moved. It was understandable. I should think they were all shattered. Julia was only fourteen, the boys eight and seven. It must have been terrible.' Pile it on, Annie, pile it on. I watch my sister's expression, distracted, puzzled. A wisp of fine fair hair blows across her forehead and she brushes it away.

'Nobody told me anything about it,' she complains.

The bird people are leaving. 'We should go too,' I say.

We do. Outside is thin watery sunshine and a brutal wind. Greta begins to talk about Rob, the children, the part-time degree she might do one day, and forgets to ask how Judith died.

Chapter Four

So here I am buying an air ticket for Toulouse. The computer in the travel agent is slow, gives me time to change my mind. I look at the racks of brochures in a sort of stupor and think of Julia. All relationships are different, differently celebrated, differently compromised, but there are duties, obligations, and these remain the same. Julia has left me her box, I must fetch it. In the end, that's all there is to it.

Outside, rain, gusts on a sharp wind. April showers ha, ha, says someone from under an umbrella. Water runs down the new granite gutter in the newly paved street. This is something we have to put up with, this prettification of our streets that only leads to wetter feet. There are hardwood bollards, tubs of bulbs to get in the way wherever there used to be open space, or anywhere wide enough to stop and talk. Nobody took human nature into account when designing all this. And a sign, to which some wag has tied a red balloon, informs us that this is a historic market town. It says much for the civic mind that they worry this is not perfectly obvious.

I nearly turn round and go back to cancel the ticket.

Wim rings.

'I'm coming over next week. I want to see what you're up to.'

41

'I'll be in France.'

'Paris?'

'Toulouse.'

David says I am wellnigh unbearable. He actually says this: 'Wellnigh unbearable.' I tell him nobody but solicitors speak like this and shut myself into the studio. I am there hours, but no good comes of it. In the late afternoon I have to come out to play mother-in-the-kitchen and there is the usual gentle rain of domestic crises, no clean shirts, no ready cash, potatoes turned green, history homework on some treaty no one has ever heard of, the phone ringing every five minutes. Much later I sit with David making a supper of toasted cheese and the remains of a bottle of Sicilian red I discovered opened in the larder. We are still a little frosty, make polite conversation.

Then Gina appears in party-going splendour and shocks us into silence and indigestion. She is four-teen, for God's sake, looks twenty. Almost twenty. But the high pale brow and bony chin that usually give her the air of a madonna by the Master of Flémalle make no impression tonight. She is all huge lined eyes and deeply coloured mouth. Her dress is silky, clinging. David's startled expression becomes heavily disapproving, but there is nothing to which he can sensibly object except the fact that his baby is now, to all intents and purposes, an adult. But she's under age, his outraged eyebrows signal, she can't buy drink, she can't have sex ... His thoughts gallop away: a fifteenth birthday party in a private house, there will certainly be drink, certainly boys. He remembers being a boy. In his day hands frequently got slapped away and girls knew how to be coy, but he remembers. His pupils widen, darken. He looks over Gina's head for help but there is

42

nothing I can do. There comes a time to realise parents are powerless.

He can't even console himself with the rarebit.

'You were always a lousy cook,' he remarks, chewing away. He likes good food nicely presented and has had to be forbearing twenty long years.

'You don't have to eat it,' I retort. This is my stock response so he looks up and smiles. When he smiles his face is more lined than ever and his eyes disappear in wrinkles. I could get sentimental over him if I cared to. I have even considered falling in love with him all over again.

'I worry about Gina,' he says feebly. He worries about Sam too but he would never let on.

'So do I. But worry gives you grey hairs and gastric ulcers.'

We are more companionable now. We share the last glass of wine. I put on some Sheppard, a soothing sound. David is not a fan of early music and is ambivalent towards all things religious, tolerating my trotting off to Mass occasionally with his if-I-were-your-lawyer-I'd-advise-you-against-it look. Now he sits in his chair politely baffled. He would prefer Brahms. Or silence.

I am sitting on the floor leaning against his knee. The fire is lit because of the cold, the rain and sleet, the vagaries of spring. Sometimes, English summers being what they are, we have to light it in June. It crackles and throws out red sparks. Light flickers over the walls of books, the shabby armchairs, the Turkey rug with its frayed ends where the old dog chewed it. On the square piano David inherited through his grandmother, and which nobody ever plays, are pictures of the children and Marion and my mother dressed for a concert, nineteen, rather beautiful, and David in a pram on D-Day. Someone must have told us this was the day it was taken or how would we know? He looks as if he knew something exciting was going on or maybe someone has held up a biscuit. These photographs, so familiar, still catch us by surprise sometimes. There is one of me, for instance, as a student which I have picked up with a pang of recognition only to find I must have been mistaken. David is feeling the same about Gina, Gina six years old and very very serious, a rabbit under one arm.

'What was Gina's rabbit called?' he asks.

'Rabbit.'

'Poor thing. Didn't anyone ever tell her to support its back legs?'

'A thousand times probably.'

Pause. He wants to say something else, on another subject. His leg taps up and down.

'I'm glad you've changed your mind about France.'

'Are you? But you had no idea why I didn't want to go.'

'You wouldn't tell me.'

'I'm not sure I knew myself.'

He doesn't believe this. He presses his lips over the words that might escape. 'I can't offer to come,' he says firmly after a while. He means big girls must manage on their own, must cope with any nonsensical internal angst. Besides, he has spent months looking forward to the New York trip, a top-drawer conference for the sort of thrusting lawyer he most definitely is not. He is going there to meet a New Hampshire friend who definitely is, and they will enjoy their brief time away from responsibility, behaving badly in dinner jackets. It will be an opportunity to forget wives, teenage daughters, sons who have given up places at Harvard or who are about to chuck architecture to become bodgers or Buddhist monks.

'I wouldn't want you to come,' I tell him truthfully.

'I suppose,' he begins. He gives me a sly look. 'What happened in the Cevennes? You never said.'

'Julia's mother drowned.'

'Drowned where? How?' Now he has his legal mind at work.

'In a river. She just slipped and fell in. It was the sort of place you could slip, narrow, a lot of rocks. The boys were always being told to keep away.'

'The boys?'

'Julia's brothers.'

'Nobody near? Nobody to pull her out?'

'Nobody.'

'And?'

'And nothing. It was just a tragedy. Tragedies happen to lots of families. I was hustled home, tidied away, you might say. What else could they do with me? I was just a child after all, Gina's age.'

'Gina.' He looks at his watch, hoping it is time to ply his taxi service, snatch her from the drink and the dancing and all the dangerous young men like the young man he once was. He leans to poke the fire, needing to relieve his feelings.

'Did you dress like that at fourteen?'

'God, no. Cotton frock and socks, those awful English school sandals. My mother would have died if I'd used lipstick.'

'Why aren't we like that now?' he wonders.

'*Autres temps, autres moeurs*,' is my trite reply.

The day I leave for Toulouse is the day the sun finally shines properly and they turn out the cattle on the Common and there are two herons fishing our side of the river. The air is intensely warm and full of the smell of growth. I have packed a bag and my artist's box which I won't need. 'Take it,' says David. 'There's sure to be something to paint.' There speaks

45

the fisherman always certain of a trout. You don't understand, I want to say. But how can he when I don't tell him?

I could never paint St Vierge.

Sam is driving me to the airport, a wretched journey from here, not undertaken lightly. He is borrowing his father's car and looks grave and responsible. Coming home he will throw off these restraints and probably be stopped for speeding. Gina hangs about offering advice on clothes. 'Have you enough? I thought mountain nights were freezing?' In a minute she will be urging me to go out for some Viyella pyjamas. She sounds like a mother.

David pecks me goodbye, dashes off. In a few minutes Greta will arrive for Gina who is torn between wanting to go – Greta's house being more luxurious and exciting than this one – and wanting to stay with Sam who, she declares, will bring home girls every night and never clean the sink. I wander about unnecessarily making sure doors are locked, the cat is fed, there are not too many private emotions on show in the studio. I linger here, willing Greta to come. Julia is still turned to the wall, but I have put the preliminary sketches of the little girl at the piano on the easel and these too mean a great deal, expose me. Painting from life is an intimate business. In this picture, among other things, perhaps I am remembering that I am the child of a concert pianist turned teacher, a child with no competence for this, the most important thing in her life. Notes on a page meant nothing to me. But when she played ...

'Annie, there you are. I thought I'd never get here,' and Greta bursts in. She never enters anywhere quietly, loves to create drama. 'Lorry overturned on the bypass. Dunne's Corner. Chaos.' She is excited. The ritual of the domestic day has been disrupted.

46

'Have fun.' Gina kisses me. Then suddenly, at the last minute, wants a clinging embrace like a toddler.

'Come on,' says Greta. 'We're late.'

'Isn't Aunt Greta always late,' remarks Sam as they take off up the street violating exhaust emission laws and speed limits. 'That car ought to be seen to, it belches black smoke.'

'It's nearly new, complies with every one of nine hundred regulations.'

'It still belches black smoke.'

'See you,' says Sam. He kisses me, turns round abruptly, leaves.

They are calling the flight and I am nearly the last passenger through. Everyone else looks bored or tired or both. The plane is half empty. Toulouse in March is not a popular destination. I look out as the runway blurs and falls away and we lift and are flying.

But I have been flying for days, flapping helplessly against cold streams of air from the past.

Oh damn you, Julia.

Artists are understood to be complex, sensitive beings. Or bloody-minded, have it how you will, David says. He does not care for mysteries and this creation thing is a mystery, the creators suspect. He walks warily in galleries and at arty gatherings, like a landsman among sailors; he acknowledges they have some kind of arcane expertise, but thinks they make too much of it and is certainly not going to be made to feel deprived because he does not share it. Once I introduced him to my first real teacher, a man of some fame and numerous cultivated eccentricities, and all he could say afterwards, with a bleak look, was 'I wouldn't leave my daughter alone with *him*.' This was in the days before he had a daughter so I laughed harshly and said

47

I didn't understand him, Will was really a shy man, confused even, gentle, the affectations were to hide behind. A tall man with a great belly, a beard, a tendency to wear sweaters with plate-sized holes. What had he taught me? That nobody teaches anybody to paint anything. They show you ways and means and then, like parents with children, they must stand back and let go. If you can you will, if you can't ... Well, computer design perhaps.

Technique fascinates me. I have yet to get a bloom on a grape that I approve. People who think art has already gone well beyond this point assume I am a madwoman, treating me gently and with circumspection. But I am still after the grape. It isn't that I want to spend my life painting bowls of fruit, but that I want to be able to paint other things with the knowledge of the pear's speckled skin, the grape's bloom, in my brush. This is difficult to explain.

Such obsessions do not worry David and he rarely pretends to understand them. He deplores my prowling in the small hours mixing blues and reds and apparently only achieving sludge brown and hysterics. And light: why am I always experimenting with light? he asks. Oh can't you see, look at the way it falls, informs, exposes. Look how many ways it can be conveyed to the eye that sees or thinks it sees a piece of perfect realism. Hazardous realism.

I have taken out my sketchbook and am drawing a small child – ten, eleven? – hanging over a gate. Julia? The face is obscure. She is holding a long stick and is poking at the ground. Perhaps Gina. Perhaps Julia as I imagine I saw her once, as I did see her once. The stewardess, bringing food, waits patiently while I put everything away, says, 'That was nice. D'you illustrate books?' Later, in the mirror, I look hard at this middle-aged woman, hair tamed into her nape, charcoal suit, red silk scarf, and wonder if this is what book illustrators look like. I wish I had come in something more casual, something for airports, hire cars ...

When my mother took us to France for holidays there were no motorways, just straight empty roads between avenues of trees. Every other small town it would be market day. We went slowly, were diverted, in every sense, filled the car with crumbs from daily picnics, were rained on by the greasy northern rain, explored Laon in a sea of mist, were mudbound near Peronne, sat on empty beaches in Normandy, climbed the towers of obscure castles, took hesitant part in baroque church services. My mother spoke fluent, tumbling French, her tenses all singular and present but her vocabulary large and vaguely operatic. Once we met, in some tiny hotel, a violinist who had heard her play long ago in Berlin. He kissed her hands and was complimentary. She was already a little drunk and became suddenly a stranger, charmingly flirtatious. Later she played Chopin for him on an old upright. People crammed in from the bar to listen. I remember the applause which made me glad for her, glad she had an audience again. And then Tottie in the doorway, shoving through the men's legs, the women's black skirts, a small determined figure in pyjamas. 'Mummy? Mummy. Mummy.' Each time a higher note.

Looking back I see how brave of her it was to set off in a chancy vehicle with two small daughters and a Michelin guide. She was not naturally adventurous. Or perhaps she was, but in the dreary struggle to make a living her courage failed her. Still, we saw Coutances and another year Chartres itself. I held her hand. She carried Tottie on her other arm.

I close my eyes.

*

49

It is late afternoon and I am driving down back roads, keeping on the right as instructed by the officious pimply youth who gave me the keys of the car. I am catching sight, briefly, of that old self-assured France where cows and geese could slow one down and mechanical failure was put right with cheerful ingenuity by rural mechanics who had never before seen under the bonnet of a Humber. Neither England nor France is self-assured today, they are brash and strident and generally dirty. They swagger, but have lost their way. So where are we all going? Where am I going? Why aren't I at home in my Aelbert Cuyp? I'm lost and tired and hungry. In Greta's kitchen Gina will be sitting down to a good meal, the dogs in their baskets, the cousins coming in and out.

An avenue of trees, a turning ... Is this the place? My mother used to drive with a map propped on the dashboard, so did Judith on that long journey to St Vierge. Judith. I sat behind her all the way. If you asked, I could draw the clasp of her pearl necklace, mix you the colours of her hair. We stopped for meals I remember, once a restaurant where we tackled some river fish with startling bones and a surly waiter who resented bloody roastbeefs. At some point, as her anger rose, Judith's hairpins began to slip out. In five minutes her hair was down her back. Blushing, furious, she scattered coins over the bill on the table, said something – rude? – and hurried us into the street.

I am here, turning into a drive, and I am there, scuffling across the gritty tarmac to the car under the limes, the boys lagging behind, squabbling, Julia in front, aloof. I am wishing I was at home, somewhere familiar and safe. The car is hot when we reach it and though we open all the windows it remains hot, makes us all feel a little sick.

I am here, ringing a bell at a pleasant shuttered

house, and I am there, Judith's hair in my face as I lean forward. 'Are we nearly there yet?'

'Madame, welcome,' says Monsieur Chartier, coming to the door. He is very formal, tall, thin with an old man's thinness, bony and slack. As we enter he calls 'Monique! Monique,' in a confident voice as if to indicate to her that I am not quite as dreadful as she supposed.

She takes her time appearing, none the less. She is a small woman in black silk. Her face is sharp: beaky nose, little pointed chin, dark wary eyes. She has about her a general air of contempt. I wonder what it is about the box that so upsets her, the box or Julia's troublesome request it should be given to me. I am not expecting an embrace, hold out my hand, but she grasps it strongly, offers a papery cheek.

'So, this is Annie,' she says.

Chapter Five

We are already in the mountains. The air, even at mid-morning, has a chill. Monsieur Chartier has driven here very carefully, as if conveying eggs, at any rate something delicate, possibly distasteful. On the way, because the silences are getting longer, he tells me Monique's brother was a university professor, now runs a bookshop. He is younger than Monique, he says with emphasis, as if this explains something. We reach a small town, remote, apparently unspoiled except by a rash of new shops in the centre for which the inhabitants no doubt said thank God and who cares about the architecture. I am expecting any minute to pull up at a solid bourgeois house suitable for an academic and a bookseller, but we drive on, round bends, into woods. There are steep wooded drops, steep wooded peaks. Then we turn off the smooth tarmac on to a bumpy track and begin to descend. More woods. We seem to be falling down the side of a valley. At the bottom will be water. Suddenly emerging from the trees we rattle another fifty yards to stop by an old mill house, discreetly restored. There is the smell of wood smoke.

'We have arrived,' says Monsieur.

We get out and stand in uncomfortable intimacy on

the doorstep. He does not knock but opens the door and calls. There is the muffled barking of a dog, the hurried click of footsteps.

'Armand.' He is enveloped in a floury hug. She has been baking, sleeves rolled up, fingers all pastry. For a moment he relaxes, all smiles. She is being careful not to mess up his jacket, but is obviously affectionate, telling him he looks thinner, asking after Monique.

Then they turn to me.

'Please call me Annie,' I say.

The woman, wife of Monique's brother, is tall, long-legged, big-nosed and elegant. Her gaze is shrewd. She doesn't bother to conceal her conclusions: that I look harmless, have no dress sense. We repair to the kitchen and here is the brother in a wheelchair. He holds out a square brown hand. He has soft thick hair like a boy's but it is grey, it looks as though his wife cuts it herself with the kitchen scissors. I think that a wheelchair in an old mill must be awkward, but then notice there are none of the steps I expect. All smoothed away in the rebuilding. It has had to be rebuilt, Denise tells me, it was just a ruin when they found it. She takes me to see the view from the living room, floor-to-ceiling strips of glass beyond which is a raging torrent. Always a lot of water this time of the year, she says, and holds up her floury arms in resignation.

Then she takes me to a stark, absolutely spotless bedroom. The floor is beautiful polished wood.

'I understand you're an artist,' she says.

'I paint portraits.' I hear myself being offhand. 'Tell me, how old is the mill?'

After this, at some fairly advanced hour, we eat lunch. Julia is not mentioned. The box is not mentioned. Later I feel warm enough to risk a walk outside to see the torrent. There is a cold wind and an all-over wetness. We are deep in the valley, sheltered

from storms but at the mercy of the river and its drift-
ing spume. I stand and look and shiver and try not to
think about Judith, which is ridiculous, I've come here
to think about these things: Judith, Julia, Alain ...
Was this the river then? Twenty miles into the hills
does this water pour below St Vierge?

'Madame. Annie. Come in, please. So cold. We're
always the last to see the spring down here in the
depths. Come in. It does terrible things to the lungs.'
Denise, a coat over her shoulders, is standing on the
bank.

I come in. I find a fire roaring in a great stone hearth.
The men are talking wild boar and casting aspersions on
local politicians. I sit with them and am asked about
England, so far north, such irrational people. Julia has
not explained anything apparently nor attempted to
reconcile them to us. After a while a sense of unreality
prevails, I feel I am in a dream. David and Gina and
Sam are far far away, scarcely remembered. I am alone
here, coping in a baffling grown-up world, catching
glimpses, noting patterns, feeling my way.

As I did once before, at fourteen, at St Vierge.

Julia, where are you?

Julia and Philippe died together in a car crash. It is
Jean-Paul, the brother, who tells me. He is astonished
I do not know already. He goes on to describe it all
coolly, it happened more than two months ago and he
has been through it many times before. His only
gesture is a sudden swooping of the hand to indicate a
vehicle leaving the road, falling. There are plenty of
places to fall off the road in the mountains, he says
bleakly.

Shock. Why didn't I ask how she died on the phone,
or as soon as I arrived? All along they have assumed
I knew.

I am sitting at the table in the kitchen. The man in the wheelchair is opposite. My chest feels tight. Jean-Paul is not being melodramatic in any way, far from it, but I keep seeing that movement of his hand, imagine the brakes failing, the car sliding, the dreadful edge, the plunge, an explosion. But Julia's car, a new Fiat, had not exploded, had wedged itself between trees, crumpled but complete.

'I didn't know any of this,' I tell Jean-Paul. He can hardly believe this, he thinks women naturally curious. And Julia my friend ... Slowly, speaking very quietly – in case Armand should come in? – he begins to fill in the background. This too he has been over many times, over and over perhaps in the long nights, comforting Monique for the loss of her only child. Was this why she wouldn't come? Such memories here in the mountains.

Julia and Philippe had been to dinner at a friend's house. Julia had not been keen. It was a dark winter night, not a host she cared about. There had been some paltry tiff, an atmosphere. So what? Husbands and wives must be allowed to behave badly. Otherwise it was a good evening, good conversation, good food, nothing out of the ordinary. But I get a vague impression of an uneasy marriage, Julia being difficult. They'd been married ten years, had no children. No explanation for that and nobody's business but theirs anyway. They were often abroad, did some skiing, sailed, enjoyed a sophisticated night life when in Paris or New York. What time did they have for children? Besides, too late now, Julia as old as me and not likely to suddenly turn maternal. A disappointment for Monique possibly, no grandchildren.

'She was chic, Julia,' says Jean-Paul. He sits back in his chair, easing his shoulders, smiling. He is smiling at a memory. 'Chic,' he says again. He is saying she could pass for a Frenchwoman, no big northern bones, no high-pitched voice, no ungainliness. She knew how to dress, and eat, and value herself. *Sur de soi*, he says. He liked that. He rather liked Julia though he will not say so, she wounded his feelings by long periods of withdrawal, of absurd prickliness. Now and then, he confesses, she was just a child. And where had Philippe found her? In Paris. Well, he hardly knew how it happened, but it happened. When they came down south they were already married. Naturally Monique was put out. Upset? You know how it is. She lived for Philippe. But Julia was all right, good stock, spoke French with just enough accent to be charming. A beautiful woman really. Everything could have been much worse.

Then they bought St Vierge. Jean-Paul is still surprised by this. A remote, ancient place, and so high in the hills. It needed a million francs spent on it. Not Philippe's sort of place at all. At first everyone took it for a joke. Even Monique laughed. Hardly handy for Paris, was it, and Julia not a woman to live there happily alone, half a mile from the nearest neighbour. Still, there is was, it was what they wanted apparently.

'What Julia wanted?' I ask.

'What Julia wanted, Philippe wanted,' he says.

Denise comes in. Did I sleep well? Would I like more coffee? Only twenty miles to the house so no hurry and tonight, well, for however long, the bed is there, the mill is to be considered home ... You understand? I understand. Even so, she is holding something back. Last night, for instance, several times I caught her looking at me curiously, frowning a little. What is this woman, this Annie? Is she afraid I too, like Julia, bring disruption and tragedy? She has a marvellous bony face, great eye sockets, that proud jutting nose. I would like to paint her.

'This box,' I say to Jean-Paul when she has gone to

see where Armand is. This silly box. It is like the mysterious casket given to the youngest daughter, the slighted one, by the old lady in a fairy tale. And what she must understand, among other things, is that even good magic can be unpredictable and easily abused, people drown in too much porridge or in heaps of gold coins.

'The lawyer will meet you at the house. Everything's arranged. Denise will put you up a picnic. There's no knowing ... He's not always punctual.'

Why does all this rigmarole have to be gone through, I wonder. Why at St Vierge?

'It would have been more convenient for all of you if I'd just picked up the box in Toulouse.'

'But the lawyer has the key and keeps a tight fist. You thought we had it? Ah no. And there have been several small difficulties, debts, a bank loan on the property, the furniture that was my grandfather's and Monique would liked returned. Family pieces, she says, lent, not given. And these legal types like to spin things out, don't know how to hurry, they spend lifetimes learning not to ... So, we jog along. And the drive to St Vierge is picturesque, you'll like it.'

I imagine him driving there – no, being driven by Denise presumably – to check the locks, water pipes, any livestock. He must have done it many times recently. He cares nothing for the picturesque. He looks jaded as he speaks. He will be glad when the place is sold and they can begin to forget it, forget the road leading to it off which Julia's car skidded and plunged.

Denise comes back, pours me more coffee without asking. She talks gardening. She thinks it scarcely credible I grow artichokes and fennel and figs in my oh-so-cold English garden. Then Armand appears, pinkly new-shaven, and the men repair outside to 'see

57

to' the car or whatever, the wheelchair going at a great rate.

'Did you like Julia?' I ask Denise. No time for beating round bushes, I am off to St Vierge in ten minutes.

'Julia?' She sits very still. Then she says, 'The lawyer ... Never on time. Always hurrying in with some excuse just as you've decided he's not coming. You may be all afternoon hanging about. Shit of a man.' It's plain she has suffered this along with Monique, who has suffered enough. 'Julia? I don't know if I liked her or not. She wasn't easy to know. And she muddled attention with love, thought they were the same thing. If Philippe wanted a weekend away, a day's fishing, if he had to go on a long trip and didn't particularly want her along, then he was neglecting her, he didn't care any more. He bore it well. A sticker, our Philippe. And he loved her. Just recently though I think he began to resent it.'

'Do you know what's in my box?'

'Nobody does. If only. Monique is quite anxious about it, heaven knows why. Losing Philippe has unhinged her a little. I don't think there were any family jewels Philippe could have given away, and if he had, why should Julia leave them to you? She hardly ever wore jewels, certainly didn't covet them. It's just Monique ...' A long look. Am I going to contradict any of this? 'She thinks Julia was drunk, shouldn't have been driving, bloody selfish as usual and careless into the bargain, new car, wet road, pitch-black night, laying into Philippe for taking her to a party she didn't want to go to and hadn't enjoyed. You know. The sort of thing you think when you wake at two in the morning and the dark's full of bogeymen. Nobody knows what really happened. That's the trouble. How can anyone grieve properly with all those doubts? Perhaps Monique thinks your box holds the answer.'

'How could it?'

She lights a cigarette. 'How could it. It might even be empty. Have you thought of that?'

It is a miserable drive, wipers going, spray from lorries everywhere, my French vocabulary nearly exhausted. The verbs fall away first, then everyday words like pavement and flower. This is worse than awkward as Armand wants to talk politics, he has just heard some news on the radio which has upset him. Some woman in the Agricultural Ministry. He wants to know why the British are always being obstructive.

Rain and trees, wet and dark woods. Whatever is going on in Paris, in London, is very far away. All around are dramatic slopes, then a sign that we are in a national park or some such. I can't tell if anything is changed, I hardly saw much all those years ago. I only left the house to go to the village. But rocks don't change, the jagged outcrops. Relax, Annie, nothing to remember here. Clunk, clunk of the wipers, a sudden swerve as we nearly miss the turn. A winding lane with potholes. Do I remember this? Why should I? It was July when I came, hot sun, a resiny smell of the woods. Another turn and we are climbing. This seems familiar. A small house above a bend. Yes, that was where the old woman lived who brought us the goat cheese, Arlette's aunt.

Arlette, Alain ... What happened to Alain? He married, silly. He had children. He is retired in a nice house, plays with his grandchildren now, meets friends in the evenings for a drink, never remembers ...

'*Voilà*,' says Armand. He turns left on to a dirt track. We bump along, grinding in second gear. His expensive Renault doesn't care for it, this Deux

Chevaux surface. It doesn't do to have a thoroughbred when you need a mountain pony. Trees jerk by, dripping and swaying. There are craters filled with water. 'All this belongs to the farm up there,' says Armand. 'Blanchard. Only an old woman there now. Never anything done about this road. Well, how can she? Must be eighty, not in good health, no money. Who'd want to live in the back of beyond? I told Philippe. This place is a liability, I said. But Julia ... They must have it.'

Suddenly a smoother surface. We have crossed a boundary. Someone has levelled here and put down good stones. Then I see the house, the first glimpse, nearly all roof because of the way it is set into the side of the hill. There are the farm buildings, low, crouching. They have been repaired – sentimental to say ruthlessly – and no doubt housed the Mercedes and Julia's Fiat. There is that air of straightening up many renovations have these days, builders hate things to sag though they've sagged successfully for three hundred years.

I get out.

It is March and not July. The rain has stirred up a sharp left-over winter smell from earth and leaves. I recognise everything and nothing. It is like a dream one has dreamed before but this time there are subtle differences, a sense of panic.

'Here we are.' He has taken out the key, the iron one Arlette used to hang on the peg by the hearth. 'Come in out of the wet. It'll be cold inside, of course.'

The smell of an unlived-in house, quite distinct, but not the smell I know, that compound of damp stone, wood smoke and the baking of bread for generations. Somebody has been at work here with enthusiasm and an architect. There will be concealed lighting and a sound system. There is everywhere more light than I remember and signs of urban affluence. Grandpère's antique furniture is perfect for a Parisian banker but is too grand for this house. I feel sad for it, tarted up.

'Such rain ... What bad luck for you,' and Armand is peering out. 'There is a fine view from up here, you know.'

I find nothing to say. I am just a stranger who has strayed in out of the weather. I don't feel I have ever been here before.

'Did you hear a car?' He turns, hurries out. He will be relieved to get this over, get home.

After a while he returns with a small man the spit of Napoleon. Arnaud, the lawyer, he says. There are formal greetings. I stand like a polite child at a party waiting for her present, the little bag of ... Of what? I must look a little mad. My hair has curled with the rain and is an odd colour these days, neither red nor grey. And I'm wearing my glasses. I don't look my best certainly, don't feel my best. I want to go home. I want my present for coming all this way and behaving myself, then I want to go home.

Napoleon smiles and chatters away. Armand assures him I speak perfect French, but perfect, and stares at me helplessly hoping I might prove it. Then the legal briefcase is opened, papers are extracted, an envelope. Everything is done properly, must be seen to be done properly. More talk. The lawyer declines to stay for coffee which is as well, it is already lunchtime.

'Madame,' says Arnaud grandly and hands me the envelope. There is a word written on it: Annie. I know the writing. Annie. That big A, the rest cramped and diminishing.

There is a pause. I wonder what I am supposed to say. Why should I thank the lawyer? It is Julia I have to thank, Julia who wrote my name on the envelope in

61

which is the key to the box. When did she do this? A
few months ago? Years? Juliaaa ...

Napoleon says goodbye. Armand sees him to the
door. They both look disappointed. They were hoping
I would rush to open the box, reveal all. I feel
unnerved, disembodied. How silly. What is there to be
afraid of? Nothing. It is just these little fingers from
the past, reaching all this long way, brushing my skin.
Annie, Annie ... Look, the box is a perfectly ordinary
box and here in my hand is the perfectly ordinary key
to unlock it.

'That man,' says Armand, coming back. 'Philippe's
choice. Not local. Hates it up here. Charges so much an
hour he thinks he's God. And this house,' and he glances
around, shudders. 'A mistake from the beginning.'

'It was beautiful once,' I say.

He doesn't notice the past tense. He has no idea I
have been here before.

'They were never happy here,' he tells me.

Chapter Six

There are brass initials on the box: C H A Hawsley for certain, Caroline or Charlotte or Catherine. Julia's great-great-aunt or great-grandmother. The mahogany has been well polished, lovingly polished, over one and a half centuries.

'I'll go and fetch the picnic,' says Armand. He tries to smile but is embarrassed. The thought of picnicking in this house is absurd, so cold, so uncomfortable. And outside the dreary rain is falling and the hills are hidden in smoking mist. He is an old man and I am a stranger. He will have to report to Monique and what will he say? She hardly spoke, wasn't interested in food, didn't tell what was inside.

What is inside?

I sit at the desk and pull the box towards me. Come on, Annie. You've come a long way for this. Nothing to it. Turn the key, lift the lid. There now, nothing so frightening after all.

The box is full of letters, unmarked envelopes, photographs. Stuffed down the side a little soft leather bag of something. I don't touch it. I don't touch anything. It is all just paper, bits and pieces. I feel a huge relief and total incomprehension. What is all this *for*, Ju? I stare down and only after a long time realise I am staring at myself. On top – because she has been expecting me, hasn't she – is a photo of young Annie in a garden, a dumpy child in shorts and very English sandals. The day is obviously hot. Young Annie's plait has been skewered up on her head for coolness. She looks flushed and impatient waiting for Julia to finish – but also resigned – Julia would never be hurried. She is certainly not smiling, not saying cheese. She is squinting though, not wearing her specs. Such a tiny black and white snapshot, in focus but a little tilted like all Julia's compositions. A split second in time, an instant. My friend Annie at Charleshall, 1960.

There ought to be a note, a word from Julia. Instead there is this enigma, my picture on top of successive layers of ... I don't know what. I lean forward, making out old postmarks, the ragged edges of opened envelopes, half a word on a postcard: ELLY and an improbably blue sea. I'm aware of the front door slamming, Armand coming in from the car. He is fed up with the rain, the awkwardness, the horror of having to unwrap food and share it with an uncouth Anglaise who doesn't know how to dress and thinks the EU is a joke. He will be glad to take her back to the mill and then to the airport.

My eye falls on a packet labelled 'Summer '66'. Inside are photos big and small, some dog-eared. Are they in order of importance? Probably not. Just dumb Annie hoping for a pattern, hoping to understand. There is Judith down by the river, sitting near the rock from which she was to fall. She is much younger than I am now and is happy, smiling as one smiles at someone much loved, a man, a child. Her hair falls over one shoulder, perhaps she has pulled it there out of nervousness; attention always made her self-conscious. She wears a cotton dress, strappy shoes. And now I can hear her voice.

'If Annie wants to swim of course she can. Just

because you don't want to. Oh Julia, do try harder.'
She meant try harder to behave well, fourteen is too
old to run whining when friends don't want to play. At
this point I was somewhere supposedly out of earshot
and feeling vaguely triumphant. I was going to swim
in the *bassin* and Julia could come with me or go elsewhere, I didn't care. Not caring made me feel cheerful
and courageous. I did not even think about the snakes.

Perhaps, when I went in to put on my swimsuit,
there was Alain. A big man. Like David, I suppose. Is
there any significance in this? But unlike David, Alain
is dark and with a heavy wrinkled face, a kindly man,
usually smiling, very French. No, I can't explain what
I mean by very French. Something about the mouth,
the nose. When I was with him I was pitched uncom-
fortably between child and woman, gazing at him in
unself-conscious adoration one moment, the next
shivery and confused. I would stumble about my verbs
and make a fool of myself. He pretended not to notice,
coming to sit beside me on the low wall under the
mulberry. He was patient and funny, never patronis-
ing. I basked in his tenderness, feeling breathless as if
I had been running.

He had been one of two doctors in the village and
lived in a big old crumbling house in the road to the
church. He wore corduroys usually and threadbare
jackets. 'Like his father, the old doctor,' said Arlette.
'No soap-and-close-shave, suit and polished-shoe man,
thank God.' And how had Judith met him? 'They'd
only been here two days, the first time,' Arlette told
me, 'before it was all wild bee stings and boo-hoo.
The doctor was up here straightaway and has been
coming ever since.'

She may have glanced sideways to see how I took
this. I don't remember. She had a delight in pretended
slyness, polishing up pointed remarks like knives.

'Arlette is always scrubbing,' Judith said once, sounding vexed. 'She's always behind with the meals.' Sometimes she helped prepare vegetables, made the salad. Then Arlette would begin on the neighbours, bringing up bits of tittle-tattle, rubbing in the emphasis. *She* this, *he* that. 'If you take notice of Arlette the village is a den of iniquity,' I heard Judith tell Alain one evening. 'But I hear nothing about you. She won't say a word against you.'

Julia spoke against him, briefly, bitterly. 'That man,' she would say. 'He's always here.' Now and again she would condescend to swim, usually when Judith was out. Even in the hottest part of the day the *bassin* was deep and chill. I was always glad no part of it was more than a kick and a splash from the stone rim. We kicked and splashed a great deal but apart, avoiding each other. It was as if our old affection was ebbing away. Afterwards, when we ran up to the house to throw ourselves down in the shade of the mulberry, she would say, 'I wonder where they've gone today?' And then, 'She's always going to places with him.' Florac, Ganges, perhaps as far as Avignon. They would be in some pavement café, pleasantly tired after all the walking. In my imagination I sat them at a round green table in the shade, gave them a *citron pressé* apiece, a guidebook they pored over, heads together.

I knew Julia was jealous of her mother in some peculiar way. I didn't understand but I accepted it, it was a fact of life like her dark hair, my raging ginger. People could be infinitely strange. I had learnt that. They are born strange or they become so, they have hidden places where who-knows-what emotions are bundled, where no one else is welcome. Julia had a great many of these places. My mother said she was rather spoiled, though the word was inexact and she would often add, 'poor Julia,' while looking grave and sympathetic. I found this absurd. How could Julia be spoiled? If anything, she was quite obviously neglected. Nobody ever seemed to take much notice of her. At Charleshall Judith was abstracted, physically busy but mentally absent. She never asked questions, never reprimanded, appeared only to preside at meals or kiss the boys goodnight. The Major came and went on his mysterious errands, seldom spoke, never showed signs of affection. So who was there to spoil Julia? Only Dukie in the housekeeper's room with the tin of ginger biscuits and the knitted cat tea-cosy.

Julia took out her resentment, if resentment it was, on the boys. The boys were much younger and were therefore vulnerable. Tormenting them, she became quite vicious. She would push or pinch, break their small treasures, spoil their treats. Tim and Georgie. They are here in a photograph, chubby, innocent. One is holding a pointer by its collar, the other clutches a rabbit. It is summer. It is generally summer in photos.

I go back to Judith by the river. The river is at the foot of the hill and is forbidden. There is a narrow gorge, rocks, deep pools. There are places to knock oneself unconscious and drown. The boys, disobeying orders, play bandits among the trees, but even they are careful, never go near the edge, keep away from the narrows where the water foams and boils.

'Madame? Annie.' Armand is in the doorway. I put down the picture of Judith, close the box. Looking away, he asks, 'Is it what you expected?'

'I didn't know what to expect.'

I follow him to the kitchen. The room is unrecognisable: new stove, shiny tiles, relaid floor. A country kitchen as seen by city designers. Oh Arlette, if you could see it. But perhaps she would approve, I think. Perhaps this is what she longed for, sweeping up the ashes. I sit down and find home-made soup, a range of cheese and sausage. Monique has even packed fine linen napkins.

There are no ghosts here, no Judith, no Alain, no Julia. And there is nothing in the box either. Old pictures, old letters ... Damn you, Julia. D'you remember the letters I wrote you? You didn't reply. After I was hurried back to England I wrote. Twice. 'Aren't we friends?' I demanded. 'Where are you?' But I heard nothing. And then years passed, the sense of disappointment was forgotten – no, was pushed far down – I learned bravado. 'Don't bring it up again, Ma. I really don't care what happened to her.' After bravado, indifference. Or what passes as indifference. Julia, what did happen to you? An accident on a winding country road happened to her and so, at last, I have received the reply I waited for long long ago.

I look up at Armand, who is sucking up soup and keeping silent, hating this rigmarole: the drive, the lawyer, the silly little box, the improvised meal. Occasionally he lets his eye wander over the neat scrubbed kitchen, the hygienic worktops, the chic rustic cupboards. Does he know this was where Judith died?

No.

But Julia knew. So why did she come back?

'Who will buy it?' I ask.

'The house?' Armand has been expecting praise for the soup and now sees I am miles and years away, flitting in and out of memory. His shoulders lift slowly. 'Who knows? An English family perhaps.' He looks solemn. There are already too many English in France, he could say.

'Could we drive through the village on the way back?'

'For a reason?'

68

'I wondered ... They might know at the café. A Dr Valences. Of course, he might be dead or moved away.'

'A friend? Have you been in these hills before?'

'A family friend.' I make much of family. 'I haven't seen him since I was a child.'

'As you wish.'

He returns to his soup. He is not curious. How do I know there is a café in the village? Well, why shouldn't there be a café? Is it likely a man known to my family would drink there? His spoon goes up and down, up and down. Then it stops. He looks at me. He is conscious of being watched. This bloody Englishwoman.

'But of course,' he says gently, encouragingly, as to a lunatic. 'Whatever you wish.'

I step outside, find the rain blown away. Here is the mulberry, much bigger I must suppose and lop-sided now where someone has sawn away branches to let light into the house. I touch the trunk as I pass. Judith's tree. The low stone wall is still here but beyond it a bank of iris, new, somehow wrong. Then rough grass sloping abruptly. There is the *bassin*, gloomy and dank in the mist. There are shrubs round it, it would be a prickly bother to push through them for a swim. I go on down, treading carefully because I don't have very sensible shoes, because I'm walking into the past. Down, down. I can hear water. I have been hearing it all the time but not listening. Trees now, rustling in the undergrowth. Wild boar? Still I go on down. Now I walk more quickly, thinking of Armand waiting by the car, looking at his watch, wondering whether to ring Monique and tell her the stupid Anglaise is off into the wilderness.

The path is still here, dry under the sheltering branches. That summer it was beaten hard, rang hollow as we ran on it. And suddenly here is the river, a torrent, brown, full of twigs, debris of all sorts. Here is the tree I stood under that day though the fallen one beside it has gone. Thirty years, Annie. I blink and Julia is shouting. She shouts, 'You love Annie more than me. You love Annie more than me.'

And as I did then I turn and run away, hurrying back up the path, feet slipping, breath coming harder and harder. At the top, by the iris bed, Armand is anxious. He has cast about like a baffled gun dog. His shoes are muddy. He smiles uneasily, especially when he sees my expression. It is probably staring and stupid. 'There are Things in the woods,' the boys used to say, 'but they don't eat you if you know what to say.' Only I don't know what to say. Sorry, forgive a middle-aged woman in a panic. It'll pass.

'We must be going,' says Armand.

So I carry Julia's box to the car. Julia's answer. Such a long time coming. But is she going to explain, tell me what I need to know, what I haven't wanted to know? Some things better left. Yes, I know. I know. I know.

Armand Chartier is fundamentally a kind and sympathetic man. He has just lost his only son. He holds open the car door for me with his old-fashioned courtesy and I think he looks suddenly shrunken, his hands shaky. He begins to say something but thinks better of it, gets in himself, starts the engine. He can't wait to leave this place.

I look back once.

It is beginning to rain again.

In the village we stop by the café in the square. Armand sits in the car with the engine running while I go in. Two men are playing cards with the owner, a large, greasy and suspicious man with an improbable

lisp. I ask very politely if any of them know of a Dr
Valences, young Dr Valences only he wouldn't be
young now, used to live in the old house on the bend
past the church. A silence follows this. Then someone
says, 'Of course. Alain. Good bloke. Married a girl
from Marseilles when he was forty. Late starter, eh?
He's still at the house. Retired early. Bad heart.'

The patron is still looking with those needle-sharp,
oh-God-bloody-tourists-asking-questions eyes.

'An old friend, Madame?'

'From way back.' And I thank them, retreat.

'Well?' says Armand.

I shake my head. He drives on. We pass the house
on the bend past the church but there is rain beading
on the window, I couldn't see it if I wanted to.

Chapter Seven

If art imposes order on chaos by holding up a mirror to
the world and saying look, look here, is that any
better, do you understand now? then I suppose that's
what I'm doing this evening, bits of charcoal flying
about, pencil leads snapping. I am back in Toulouse
and Monique Chartier is sitting for me. She is a reluctant sitter. I can understand that. She thinks it all might
be a joke, this portrait business. Besides, she hoped I
would stay on a night with Denise and Jean-Paul at the
mill, so *sympathique* and my own age. Monique is not
sympathique, has never been so. She sits as if carved,
her breathing barely visible, her eyes hostile. I will get
half an hour of her, no more, so I scrabble, hurrying,
and am hard on my materials.

For all this, I achieve a face.

It comes to life under my hand. My hand is now
turning an artistic grub-colour as if I've been shifting
coal and spilling ink at the same time. A proud old
beaky face glares from the paper. I get the fall of light
wrong, curse, go back, go over, grow hot. Try harder,
Annie. Concentrate. She is waiting to be polite about
the finished piece. She expects very little skill but you
are a guest in her house. She has manners. Then try
harder. Try. This is the woman who welcomed Julia as
her daughter.

My hand pauses. I look up.

'I'm not as young as I was,' says Monique. It is an oblique way of saying she is stiff, could I finish please.

I show her the sketch. It's a good likeness. Her pride is there, the rigid bearing of head on neck indicating her unwillingness to look at anything of which she can't approve. Fine eyes too. Good bone. That nose. I appreciate noses.

'Well,' she says. Nothing more. Is she secretly pleased? Perhaps it is too bold, too honest. But she is looking at me with a little more respect. Not just a weekend painter then, say the black eyes.

'Tell me about Julia,' I say. I shall not ask about Philippe.

'Shooliaa.' There it is again, that unique pronunciation. 'Attractive. Smart. A pity there were no children but now, in the circumstances ...' She spreads her bony hands, turns them over, studies her many rings. 'I always hoped Philippe ...' A pause. She had hoped many things but wasn't going to tell a stranger, especially a stranger who was Julia's friend.

'Look,' I say. 'I hadn't seen Julia for thirty years. I didn't even know she was married. I didn't know she had died. I didn't know her at all really.'

'Thirty years,' she repeats. 'And you didn't know she was married.'

I tell her how we were at school together, about Charleshall, about the Major. The Major has been dead for years. Monique has not even seen a photo of him. Nothing is said about Judith. I say Julia and I lost touch when she moved. *C'est la vie, n'est-ce pas?* It all sounds very ordinary and my voice is light, dismissive. All these things are of almost no consequence, it implies, and were so very long ago.

'St Vierge,' says Monique. 'That awful place.'

73

'Was it Julia who found it?'

'They found it together, I believe. They went to Ganges for some reason, then afterwards made off down the back roads, explored the country. I don't know how they came to St Vierge, but it was empty, the family ready to sell. What could one say? Old people's advice is never welcome. And of course they had the apartment in Paris. They were often abroad, New York, Hong Kong. Julia went every time. She'd never have stayed alone in the mountains.' Monique crosses her slender little ankles, gazes down at them. 'She was married before. When she was too young, she said. There was a divorce.' She has not been brought up to approve of this but shrugs, bites her lip in comment. Times change. *C'est la vie, n'est-ce pas?* So, we have a divorced woman, an inconvenient old house, a peripatetic lifestyle, no children.

'She could be difficult,' I say. I mean withdrawn, serious, irrational. I mean she had a feeling she was invisible to her parents. Perhaps she often was. But all I can say in French is that she could be 'difficult'.

'Unhappy? The mother died young, I understood. She was always very much self-contained, Shooliaa.'

'She was hard to know.' Hard for me, too, closer to her than anyone. The best thing was simply to accept.

'Exactly.'

Armand appears in the doorway. 'A nightcap?' He has a tray with glasses, some sort of alcohol, little buttery biscuits.

'You must be up early,' says Monique to me. She hands my sketch to her husband. 'Is this a good portrait?' she demands.

He looks at it, at her, at me.

'It is very fine,' he says dubiously.

*

74

I don't open Julia's box again. I carry it with me in a plastic supermarket bag. Armand mentions that Monique, naturally, would be interested to know if ... Well, because of Philippe ... So few mementoes ... He kisses me goodbye with an almost military formality.

'And Aunt Charlotte's mahogany writing box to my friend Annie Harmer Somerville ...' No, a legal formula surely. 'I bequeath to Annie Harmer Somerville ...' My friend Annie. She even knew the address. How? Looked it up, Annie dear. You've lived there a long time. David isn't an ambitious executive, gambolling from company to company. But how did she know about David? I knew nothing about her.

Anyway, why not write to me then? Why not say, well Annie, I know it's been a hell of a long time, but here I am and if I die there's this box of rubbish I'd like you to have. Why? Why not? Who else is there left who would want it? The boys? Tim's in Melbourne, Georgie's at sea somewhere, lives on a boat, might be in the Med, Tenerife, Bermuda. Neither of them wants a carrier bag of old papers, old memories. They don't want to be reminded, ever, of being children, of big sister. Can you blame them? Do you remember what they were like? Solemn-faced skinny things, only eleven months between them, almost twins. Dukie used to call them twins. Shrimps. Nothing to me, just nuisances. Are you listening, Annie? You're not asleep. I know you're not asleep.

Food comes. I drink the little bottle of white wine. Julia, are you there? D'you remember the sherry we drank sitting under the currant bushes? A hot day, smells of baked earth, bruised currant leaves, the wine. You'd pinched a pop bottle full from the decanter. It was rich and warm and we imbibed seriously like old men tasting a treasured vintage.

Novelty, uncertainty, giggles, then your head slipping sideways to rest against my knees. 'I feel so sleepy,' you said.

But if I scarcely knew that Julia what about the Julia I never knew at all, the Julia who went to another school, who married, divorced, remarried, drove her Fiat off a mountain road. No, the Fiat skidded off the road, it was a dark night and raining. But that Julia, that Julia ... Hell.

There is cloud over England. We bump through it to solid ground, bounce a lot, begin to taxi. There is nothing to be seen but the grey depressing fog of rain. As usual, waiting for the doors to be opened, I experience that mild sense of claustrophobia I never have while in the air. Then after the usual struggle I step through Customs with my awkward baggage and see Sam, his gawky frame draped over a barrier. He is searching the wrong crowd, perhaps wondering if, in three days, he can have forgotten what I look like. I get closer and see his bored gaze sweep the faces all round me, miss me, begin again. Ah well, mothers become invisible eventually.

'I didn't see you.' His face is bright with relief. He was starting to worry. Tit for the hundred of tat hours I've waited for him then, after rugger matches, school plays, films, gigs, expeditions.

'I shan't ask if you missed me.'

'We ran out of mayonnaise.'

'You could have bought some.'

'I made some.'

'And?'

'Dad said it would be fine for greasing the car.'

We go to find it, the car. Sam confesses he may have got a minute scratch on it while parking, nothing that shows, it can't possibly matter. Do I think David will notice? No, I don't, but don't tell him so, he doesn't deserve such comfort. Teach him to park better next time.

'Is that all it is?' he demands as I deposit the plastic bag in the boot.

'That's it.'

'A jewel box?'

'No such luck.'

'Oh well. Back to the easel then.'

'So what's in it?' asks David. He is home early and is prowling about gloomily because I'm tired and not saying much.

'I don't know.'

'Don't know?' He is genuinely astonished. 'Haven't you looked?'

'Not properly. I think it's old letters, pictures, a few keepsakes. Nothing much.'

'I don't understand you. Aren't you interested?'

He is disappointed. These artist types, says his expression. Crazy. He wishes he were back in the USA.

'How was your bunfight?' I ask.

'In another dimension. When I got back I thought I was walking about in a picture book, you know, Traditional Rhymes for Children, women in poke bonnets and children with hoops.'

'Halingford hasn't had those in a long while.'

'But you know what I mean.'

'While you've been away we've had our dramas too,' Sam tells us. 'Grievous bodily at the Red Lion, someone shooting at the swans by the weir.'

A waft of damp air, the clatter of school shoes, the thump of a school bag. Gina bursts in followed by Greta who is agog for news, of money, property in France, diamond necklaces. She lives in a Wilkie Collins world, our Tottie.

'Well?'

I disentangle myself from Gina. 'Well nothing. A few old letters, family photos. No cash.'

It takes her an instant to recover. She has driven here faster than usual on the adrenalin of curiosity.

'Then what a fuss over bloody nothing.'

'As I said all along.'

'And by the way, this girl of yours was given a detention. I didn't know schools still did detention. She scrapped with the new young commissar biology teacher.'

I look at Gina. She gives a careless grin.

'I didn't agree with something she said.'

'Biological?'

'Political.'

'I hope you weren't rude,' is David's pennyworth.

'Of course not. Only then she got aggressive.'

'Asserting her authority,' says Greta sagely.

'Aggressive.'

Sam, who is munching toast, taps me on the shoulder. 'Good to be back, eh Mum?'

One of the messages on the answerphone is from Wim. He sounds peeved, a reasonable man at the end of his tether. Where is Annie, sod and blast, don't I know what a phone is for? He has left a number to add to the list of numbers I already have. I do not recognise the code. Budapest, possibly.

His message is so long, partly because of the expletives, that it takes up a great deal of tape. I turn it off before the end.

I won't be bullied.

See you, Wim.

I sit in the summerhouse and the river slips away quietly to the sea. A still day, the rain all blown away, the birds singing. The air is sharp with the foxy scent of crown imperials pushing up and up, shaking out their fringes of narrow leaves. It mingles with the smell of tarred wood and watermint and the linseed I have spilled down my sweater. On the seat beside me is the box. I have unlocked it but not lifted the lid. When we were children I used to play a game with Tottie. I had an old pencil box with a swinging lid. Inside I would put something small and unexpected: a robin's egg, an ear of corn, a liquorice chew, ladybirds. Tottie would blow all over it in anticipation, little round face shining, fat fingers trying to be careful. She could hardly bear the suspense. Then the lid would swing, the treasure would be revealed, she would crow with surprise, delight.

So open the lid, Annie. Get on with it.

A school report, junior school, good, good, excellent, poor. A letter to the Major asking for Julia to be kept at home for a while ... disturbed .. cried a lot in class ... difficulties making friends. A Brownie certificate. An envelope full of postage stamps: Suriname, Brazil, Ethiopia. A formal studio portrait of Judith with the boys, Tim just a baby on her lap, Georgie leaning against her knee with his puckered-up what-am-I-doing-here look. Another letter to the Major: music and dancing compulsory, lunches two shillings a day. This was the school where I met Julia.

My fingers touch the little leather bag. No, not yet. Another envelope, large, unmarked. Leave that too. Here's a wedding invitation, Major and Mrs George Benson-Hawsley request ... Julia Victoria ... Charles Dunning. So he married again, the Major. A stepmother then. I lift up the wedding photo. Julia, yes, Julia with long hair, an Ophelia expression, on the arm of a nice sort of boy in morning dress. There is a bevy of small bridesmaids looking bored. The stepmother is small, rather formidable. The Major is a little behind, eclipsed. Did she make him happy? Smoothed his way perhaps, a man not used to fending for himself. Her most recent bit of smoothing has been to arrange all this, to get Julia off his hands. And the boys ... Were they smoothed away to boarding school? They are here but very much on one side, much taller, pugnacious, defiant.

This is the first time I've seen the grown-up Julia. More cheekbone perhaps, bigger eyes. She gazes out, not smiling. Someone who did not know her would say serene. I recognise the old detachment. She's not there. She's far away, hating all this, taking refuge in the stables, the tool sheds, on the rocking horse. She has spent all morning being turned and tweaked and titivated, now she has escaped.

Did she love him, Charles David Dunning?

Suddenly tired of all this I scrabble downwards. Am I expecting them? My two letters. Write to her, why don't you, my mother had said. She had found me crying in the garden. I cried rather easily in those days and I had frightened her. I can smell the wet leaves now, the dank November smell. I expect they've moved, she said. Try again. Letters will be sent on. She had put her arms about me, lightly, briefly. Later she had played to me. Later still, in bed, I had written 'If you don't reply this time I'll know you're not my friend.'

Silence.

But look, says Julia, here you are, I've replied. A little late but then life's like that, there are so many distractions, time slips by. And you know what I was like. But I'm still your friend, Annie. I was always your friend.

What I have in the box is Julia's life, is Julia. She has given me her life, not in sequence, a little hugger-mugger. What she's saying is sort it out, Annie, make

80

something of it, I couldn't. Understand. I never did.

I close the box and carry it to the house.

On the kitchen table is a note from Sam saying he won't be home till Friday, no reason. There is a telephone number not to be rung unless a matter of life and death. I go to the studio where there is a good smell of turps and oils. I'm neglecting my work. There is the piano girl to begin. I go through my brushes, touching old friends. The cat is sitting outside making faces to come in. He has a repertoire of silent mouth-openings getting bigger and bigger as his frustration grows.

Like Julia, I suddenly think.

I go and let him in.

One way or another the days are too much for me. I feel unsettled, cut adrift. It is like being in love with all the confusion, the bouts of amnesia, and none of the compensating ecstasy.

I plague David in his office at the time of day he ought to be having coffee and an almond slice. He is unavailable. Bibs gives me a chocolate digestive as a consolation prize. She has been with him twelve years now, having started as a young thing in skimpy suits, newly married. He had turned down dozens of competent women to give this child a chance. Mrs Bibby, he would say irritably for a whole year afterwards. I can't get it into her head, he would begin every other day. Now he calls her Bibs and she runs him and his partner and the computer system standing on her head. She even finds time to polish the brass plate.

'Trouble at home?' she asks.

'No, I don't have an excuse. I'm just playing truant.'

'Spring,' she says. 'Sap rising.'

'Can anything be done?'

She laughs. 'My granny said when she was a girl they dosed her with brimstone and treacle.'

I go home. I dose myself with a glass of white wine. Then I go to the studio and lock myself in and take a long time watering all the geraniums.

Chapter Eight

It is a terrible day. The wind howls and the rain sluices across the garden. Water is dashed against the studio windows in waves as the sea is dashed against a promenade. If I had a proper studio, I think, an old thought, hardly ever taken these days beyond its beginnings. I have put off having a proper studio for so long it has ceased to matter except on days like this, days when I stand at the easel and feel assaulted by the elements. In one corner is a spreading puddle, in the gusts the glass shakes ominously. Yet when we moved here this broken-down old conservatory seemed ideal. 'A studio at last!' I exclaimed naïvely as we drove away and David, in a good mood because he not only liked the house but could afford it, said, 'We'll build you a new one when we can. A year or two.' For the time being we reglazed here and there, repainted, made do. Then I was expecting Gina. Then something else, then something else. And anyway, there is nothing wrong with the studio as it is except in frost and snow and these mischievous April storms.

But I use the rain to abandon the painting.

The girl at the piano is at the stage of looking peaky and resentful, her face half finished, her hands mere blobs on the keys. She is numbingly difficult. I'll need her to sit to me again. In the sketches I've achieved her mixture of defensiveness and contempt, but the paint is messing about, the line always just wrong, the tone just too dark. I'm painting slowly too, always a bad sign. So I clean the brushes, taking time, doing a good job. Must make a good job of something. I feel unsettled still. I think about going out in the rain.

The man from next door calls. He is sorry, he has lost his key, but if he can climb over the garden wall there is a kitchen window left open. This is a welcome diversion. I give him a leg up over the wall. He is embarrassed but cheery. I can hear him sloshing about cursing at the wet. He returns, more embarrassed, less cheery. The window is too small. He can't squeeze through. Could I? I fetch steps, climb gingerly, and he hauls me over the top and steadies me awkwardly as I topple sideways into his flowerbed. The window is nothing to a slip of a thing like Annie Somerville.

After this drama he offers me coffee which I accept, to his consternation. We drip about the kitchen until he thinks of towels. I know his wife slightly, in the way these days one gets to know neighbours out at work all day. She has something to do with refugees. She is away a great deal. He looks rueful, it's something to which he has trouble accustoming himself. He says this, almost in so many words, almost in these words he is diffident and pedantic. He is a carpenter, he says. He becomes animated only when talking about wood.

'Where have you been?' demands Sam when I get back.

'Next door.' Why is it he thinks he has a right to an answer? I'm not allowed to ask him anything.

'Dad called. He said could you ring back. Urgent.'

'He probably forgot his umbrella.'

'It sounded serious.'

'One crisis after another. It must be the weather.'

He peers at me. 'A biting tone, Ma dear. Anything the matter?'

'I can't do the goddam picture,' I tell him.

One of David's wealthy clients – he has very few – died yesterday in Cologne. The police are involved, there was a mix-up, perhaps a murder, no one seems sure. David wants me to pack an overnight bag and take him to the airport. He has had German police on one line, the widow weeping on another. Bibs has brought all her diplomatic skills to bear on both, in between doling out chocolate digestives and strong tea. It is not every day there is talk of murder, drugs and the financing of terrorist organisations. Poor Will, who has been up every night with the baby who's teething, comes to the phone baffled, his voice an octave higher than usual. He relays David's messages, then David comes on to relay them again in person. He is also baffled but confesses to being irritated as well. He always thought Buckley an old buffoon, a man who dealt in property compulsively, who made conspicuous donations to local good causes, who enjoyed a councillor or two in his pocket. Not a pleasant man, but only a petty tyrant, nothing out of the ordinary. Now they are busy extracting bullets and talking big fraud, big dirty business.

At the airport David is all pessimism. He knows nothing. What help do the police expect him to be? And not just police, but those other branches of law and order, plain clothes, secret, secretive. 'Let's hope they've made a mistake,' David says, but gloomily, pushing away the coffee I have just bought him. There is almost no one about and he looks and feels in limbo, a country mouse on the way to town.

The flight lifts off on time and rapidly disappears into

85

filthy weather. I wonder if I put in handkerchiefs, his cufflinks. I'm no good at the dutiful wife thing. I take the view his underwear is his own affair. And what he really wants is sympathy, a peck on the cheek, human contact. He can buy pyjamas in Cologne.

I drive home thinking of our second-last conversation, inevitably about Julia's box.

'For God's sake,' David said. 'Oughtn't you to sort it out?'

'I'm not ready.'

'What do you mean, not ready? They're just old letters, odds and ends.'

'I'm not ready.'

We have had this exchange almost every other day in the two weeks since I returned from Toulouse. He is touchy about the box because he's touchy about Gina these days, this daughter fourteen-looking-eighteen who doesn't want to be his little girl any more. He is afraid for her and of her. He thinks he is getting old. Irrationally, he looks in mirrors more and has become a trifle loud, forbidding late nights and certain company with a vehemence quite out of character.

At home there is the afternoon quiet, broken only by the monotonous drum of raindrops on the studio roof. The puddle now fills the entire corner. I move the easel slightly as if, if this goes on, there is a danger of it becoming imperilled by rising water. It is a mistake to tamper with it, of course. The imperfections of the picture are revealed more cruelly for the sudden shift in light.

Claire. There is nothing very Claire about her, she has straight black hair and that ruthless expression of disdain. To disguise fear? Children who have ambitious parents suffer God knows how. Her father wants her touring the world by thirteen, chaperoned by him from Moscow to Los Angeles, Oslo to Canberra. Only three years to go then. Practise, child, practise. She lives, eats, dreams, delights in and despises piano.

'Weird,' is Gina's comment, crashing in from school and finding my sketches over the kitchen table. 'What a little horror.' How much of the dedication to art is hers, she wants to know, how much papa's? Impossible to tell. Genius is unpredictable, so are people. I'd like to paint the father. Fanatics have always interested me. He has a marvellous nose too, fleshy but thrusting. If I were a child he would frighten me to death.

I gather everything up and take it back to the studio.

'Give me an hour,' I say to Gina, who is boiling an egg with the sadly automatic competence of a child neglected by her mother.

'It must be damp out there,' is her parting remark, cast over her shoulder as she fiddles with the gas.

I take out the portrait of Julia and put it up on the easel.

Here she is, leaning forward. Hello Annie. Calm voice. She was never effusive. Just arrived, told to run along, I never needed to ask where to find her. You could hear the creak of the boards from the foot of the stairs. Up, up, on soft feet. Surprise her, Annie. She won't have heard the car. There are lozenges of light scattered by the panes of the great window, on the bare boards, the slowly moving horse, the dark dipped head. Hello Ju. No kissing, perhaps not even smiles. Only later would she come close, stand close, sit close, her arms brushing mine, fine hair electrically tangled in my red. The best she could do, a stranger to physical contact. I've been waiting for you, she might say. *All morning*. She is not sensible of time, not as other people, other children are. She measures in her own way. All morning means ages, aeons, a life and a half.

I pick up a brush.

I paint her over, paint her out with red. It is there on the palette, already mixed. Dark, blood-clot red. What for? Why that shade?

Why not. Good enough for painting over. The result surprises me. There are tones and half tones in the stuff and the artist was clearly agitated when applying it.

Goodbye Julia by Annie Somerville.

'Are you busy?' asks Sam, tapping gently. He has come in to find Gina worrying about not having enough to eat and the studio door is shut, hard luck. But now he is a man he likes to break rules, take sides, make unpopular decisions. He stands well back though, in case I lob a tube of oil.

'Not any more.' I emerge briskly, fingers like bloody talons.

'That's a lovely colour. Look, I'm off at seven. Gig. Gina's starving. She says one egg's not enough.'

Actually Gina has found some salad and is making a dressing. There is oil down her school sweater. 'And there is bread,' she declares triumphantly. 'And olives.'

'I forgot to shop. Your father had to fly to Cologne.'

'Where the Eau de comes from?'

'Originally, one supposes. Someone died in a shooting.'

'Someone Dad knows?' Sam is excited. He has led a quiet life and always hopes, like Greta, for a little drama.

'Time poor old Dad had some excitement,' says Gina.

Not involving guns, I say. I trust he spends most of his time drawing up wills and advising on boundary disputes. He leads a very ordinary, circumscribed life. He enjoys the local and particular. He has nothing to do with guns.

'I'm sorry about the meal,' I say.

The phone begins to ring.

'Herr Somerville,' says Sam. 'Checking up on his incompetent *hausfrau*.'

'The man they tell me about isn't the man I knew,' says David. He sounds miserable and affronted. He has been learning things he would rather not know. And his German is rudimentary, like a dog coughing.

'Is it anything to do with you?' I imagine him standing there in his socks, his shirt half-buttoned, his face creased with bewilderment. He is in his hotel room. He has scarcely been there an hour and has been interviewed twice. Now all he wants is a bath and an uninterrupted meal.

'They want to know about his investments. I told them to ask the widow. I only handled local stuff, his property, that messy business with his first wife. Heaven knows what he was doing elsewhere. But I can tell they're not keen on iffy Brits shot dead in respectable German apartments. It isn't good, not for crime statistics. EU band-of-brothers crap, or diplomatic blood pressure.'

'And the widow?'

'She's keeping quiet. Weeping's the safest thing to do probably. She's flying out tomorrow with the eldest son to identify him.'

'Didn't they ask you to do that?'

'No, thank God. I never cared for him anyway.'

'Is that relevant?'

He is silent. He is probably shifting from foot to foot. When he speaks again he sounds plaintive.

'I miss you.' As if this is a shameful thing to admit he adds quickly, 'But not your cooking.'

'I'm not doing any,' I tell him.

The bed is too cold and roomy for one. I lie in it and worry about David. What are they keeping him there for? Doesn't he look what he is, a stolid well-meaning charmingly dull man of integrity. Surely the sharp know-all *polizei* will laugh at him and send him home. Bugger fame and fortune, we are happy in our Cuyp.

I get up. It is midnight. I fetch the box, Julia's damn box, and sit up on the bed with it, a quilt round my shoulders. I take out the packet of photos from 1966. Here is Judith again by the river, here Arlette by the mulberry, self-conscious, now the boys in swimming trunks and teetering on the rim of the *bassin*. And here am I with Alain. We are rather blurred and, like Arlette, are vaguely embarrassed. He lounges against the low wall, I sit on it. Both of us look much younger than we were.

A late starter ... A girl from Marseilles ... A bad heart.

Look, Annie. A postcard of the holy well. Julia has started to write on the back but has got no further than 'It is very hot here ...' It is addressed in her careful, crabby hand to Mrs Duke, Charleshall. Dear God, what is the point of all this? A box of memories, of no importance now to anyone living. And my eye falls on the newspaper cutting, the close black print, the formal French: 'Englishwoman drowns in accident'. Well, weren't tourists always falling off mountains, being overwhelmed by avalanches, killed in road crashes? I read slowly. It mentions Alain and Arlette who searched for her, it mentions her desolate children, the neighbours who bore in the body; who were

90

they? Monsieur Blanchard perhaps was one, and the fact that Judith was thirty-six.

I won't do it. I don't want to go back. This is Julia's past, not mine. I simply flitted in and out, the maid, the spear-carrier, the dumb friend. Close the box, Annie. Forget it.

The house is quiet. Next door Gina sleeps soundly. I can close the box and put it away and that will be that. But ... But Julia has given it to me and if I don't want to be like David, confused in Cologne, I have to read and look and try to understand. This is what Julia wants. She wants me to understand.

The little bag contains three rings and a locket. It is an old locket, gold. It was Julia's twelfth birthday present from her grandmother, passed down from her grandmother perhaps. I remember Julia put it aside, jewellery did not interest her. And she had no sense of history, of family. I open it after a struggle and there is a picture, very small and faint, of ... of Annie.

One of the rings is also very old, set with pearls and lapis lazuli. The others are diamonds and diamonds and sapphires. Engagement rings? They have been bought or inherited, been given and given up, have been removed from living hands or dead ones. Now they are just pretty things on my palm, valuable yet meaningless.

Put them away.

Here is Julia about eight years old. A school photo. She is tall for her age, thin, the dark hair cut severely and pinned back. She has her secret look. She is enduring all this, getting through it. Even in a class group she is a lonely figure. None of the others is as rigid, head up, breath strictly held. They have only just stopped chattering, are suppressing grins. Friends lean together a little, the way friends do for support, to

91

show solidarity. Julia does not lean and yes, she is definitely holding her breath, willing the moment over.

I remember her at Charleshall, flying between the box hedges. It was a fine garden for hide-and-seek. She was often distracted though, grew tired of hunting, went off on one whim or another. Sometimes it was to perpetrate those small meannesses on the boys, taking the rope ladder when they were up a tree, tipping the train from the rails, putting snails in their boots. I never helped her. I always refused, scarlet, indignant. 'Ju, how could you?' Mostly all this happened while I sat, waiting for her to come. Sometimes, suspicious, I went to look for her, and she would be with Dukie eating cake or in the vegetable garden popping pea pods. Juliaaa, I would wail. Oh Julia. Aren't you playing?

Yes, she was playing. She meant nothing by it, this excursion. She felt hungry, she heard voices and went to see. Time is so elastic to her. Time was. In my head all this is the present, the years are jumbled together. There we are playing Robin Hood or lobbing pea grit at the goldfish in the round pond on the lower lawn. Charleshall is the sort of place that has upper lawns and lower ones and nut walks and wooden seats in arbours. Apart from the cousins, who came because they must, I was the only child to share all this with Julia. 'Well, I don't want anyone else. Why should I?' she said.

More photos, little crooked snaps by Judith or long-suffering Georgie, who was a keen photographer until Julia sabotaged his camera. Here we are up a tree looking dishevelled, and by the pond looking goody-goody, Julia in a dress – because she always wore one – and little Annie in shorts – because she always wore them. We are close together always but not touching. We have defensive, rather mutinous expressions. We often scrapped. Here is Julia's world-defying face, here she has not had time to stitch it on, she's been laughing. Yes, I remember her laughing. She did laugh. She could be kind.

Images rise, like the fish in that pool: sun-warmed plums, gooseberries, the creamy flesh of young walnuts, tiny broad beans in the pod. We were always eating. And there was always something to eat. Even Julia, so fastidious indoors, stuffed anything into her mouth out here, cracking hazel nuts on a stone with a quick bang of her heel, giving herself stomach-ache with too many sour little apples. Two Julias. There were two Julias. The one in the garden under the gooseberries or on the rocking horse singing softly, forwards and back, forwards and back ... And then Julia proud and cold and gone away into that inner world.

I am falling asleep.

It is so tiring, tramping these landscapes of the past. One needs strong boots, a strong constitution.

I think of David snoring gently in Cologne, a city I do not know nor probably ever shall. He will wake in the morning to the body in the mortuary, a hysterical widow, a bit more intentionally brutal muck-raking. A lot of unanswerable questions, no doubt. Who's on the Euro-fiddle now?

I turn off the light.

Don't go, Annie. Why shouldn't I? You cheated. You've been eating biscuits indoors. I've been hiding *hours*. No, don't go, Annie. Look, I've brought you some. All right?

All right, Julia.

Chapter Nine

In the morning the rain has blown away entirely.
There is a summery warmth. The swans are moving
down river on a desultory journey of exploration.

'I'm going to be late,' says Gina with relish. She has
been reading a magazine instead of eating breakfast,
yearning after glamour. 'I'd like one like that,' point-
ing to a model wearing a skinny black slip of a dress
held up by a prayer. But five minutes later she skips
off happily enough in her dowdy uniform looking no
more than twelve.

I go to the studio.

Judith said once, 'Aren't you ever lonely, Annie? I
was an only child and I was. Often.'

'But I'm not an only child. There's Tottie.
Margaret.'

'Of course. I always forget. But she's only tiny,
isn't she?'

'There's Julia,' I pointed out.

'Yes. There's Julia. How silly of me. You do see a
lot of each other, don't you?'

We were at Charleshall where Judith always seemed
so languid, so unoccupied. Preoccupied might be the
better word. She greeted people abstractedly, especially the Major, smiling only in his general direction,
hardly stopping to let him peck her cheek. There was a

coolness between them though I thought nothing of it. I had no loving parents of my own for comparison. Besides, adults were mysterious, inconsistent and absurd.

I think, in spite of everything, she coped well with the house. Meals were on time, beds changed, bathrooms properly scoured. She liked and respected Dukie, with whom she was always having to discuss grocery orders, menus, the giving of parties. In race weeks they gave big parties and a great many people would have to be put up, fed, entertained. Once or twice I saw her in evening clothes, fragilely elegant, like a shy child dressing up. She was so very slender. Like Julia.

'And *you're* fat,' said the cousins to me. 'Lumpy Annie, Lumpy Annie,' they sang out at me between the sheltering laurels along the path to the stables. They really wanted to spite Julia, but Julia was elsewhere and I was an easy target.

'You're not fat.' Julia linked her arm in mine. She bent her head so that the wings of hair brushed my skin. Close to her eyes were as grey, as pale as a winter's sky. 'You're just right.'

I was consoled. The cousins were just the cousins, silly, excitable, uncouth. I could laugh them off. Julia had condescended to comfort me, a rare and precious privilege. We smiled at each other. Who would stand up for us if we didn't stand up for each other? But then by tea-time she seemed to have forgotten, told the Lumpy Annie story to the grown-ups. Judith smiled sympathetically and immediately talked of something else. The cousins, appalled, contrite, kicked at me under the table to say sorry. My face flamed. I stared at my plate. I flamed inside too, at Julia's casual betrayal. I felt the terrible fragility of her love, bestowed and then snatched away in the course of a few hours. Friends in books never acted so cruelly, nor would the other friends I had at school. There were rules one didn't break except deliberately, to break hearts. But Julia was always strange and imperfect like someone in a fairy story. People often behaved oddly or inconsistently in such stories and either no one noticed or anyway it all turned out for the best.

'Sometimes I hate you,' I told her after tea. 'Why did you have to tell your parents?'

'Did you mind? But why should you? You aren't fat at all.'

'I know.'

'Then you needn't mind. And I thought Alex and Hatty and Sam needed showing up. Little liars.'

She had done it for my sake then. She had her own code of honour, as real as mine but incomprehensible.

'Don't hate me,' she said.

And we rocked together on the rocking horse, silently, until bed.

Here is a picture of the car. I think it was a Vauxhall. It was roomy but swayed a lot, inducing car sickness. Judith was equipped with all kinds of remedies for this but when it came to the point simply said, 'Oh, for Heaven's sake, if you must, lean out of the window.' From the moment of leaving Charleshall she had been in this careless mood, smiling, overlooking lapses in behaviour. Her hair seemed to have a golden aura about it. An absurd little white hat perched there, and she wore a navy suit, smart, not too English. On the boat people gave up seats for her.

The boys were grumpy, of course. As soon as they were confined they seemed to feel the need to tear about. In the car they threw paper pellets at each other, on the ship they vanished entirely and were retrieved by perspiring crewmen from the lower decks. North-eastern France, as always from the sea, looked disappointing, mudflats and cranes, industrial greyness, drizzle. I don't mind. I've seen it before. I eat a sandwich and drink tea from Judith's thermos and am phlegmatic, comfortable. My mother never allowed panic or tantrums or disappointment on holiday. She taught me how to change the wheel on the Humber and make the Spanish omelette which we take, cold, to keep ourselves going if all the restaurants are closed. I was a seasoned and philosophical traveller. 'If only they were like you,' murmurs Judith with a sideways glance at her mutinous crew.

We spent the first night not too far from Calais. To give us time to adjust perhaps. Julia seemed miserable. Judith sparkled. The next day she was in green and dashed along overtaking slow lorries and old men on bicycles. She and I sang songs: 'One Man Went to Mow', 'The Marseillaise', 'John Brown's Body'. Now and then there were cows in the road or a horse and cart. Somewhere we stopped for coffee and a cake. 'Funny cake,' complained Georgie who was inclined to miss home comforts. At the café table we peered at the map, but France was a blur of saints' names and hyphens. Then on we went past brown cows and black cows and women in headscarves and quiet shuttered towns and isolated châteaux.

That evening Judith was more animated then ever. She looked even younger. Julia was cross, she said people were looking in the restaurant. Mothers oughtn't to dress like girls, she said. Could Judith have been mistaken for an elder sister in her white dress scattered with poppies, her pretty white shoes? I remember that as she grew happier and lovelier, Julia grew more sour. Her frowns deepened, her squabbles with the boys grew more prolonged. She refused breakfast before we set out on that last day and then complained of hunger at ten o'clock. She made a mistake in the navigation which I thought was deliberate. But by then we had reached the mountains, the chestnut trees, the oaks and pines, the stone farms, the steep towns, the ravines. Judith no longer bothered with directions. She drove swiftly, daringly, not looking over her shoulder. Not looking back for Julia, for the Major, for that other life.

At last the bumpy track, a glimpse of roof, chimneys, a thread of smoke. It was late afternoon and growing cooler. There was the chill of the heights.

'St Vierge,' said Judith in triumph.

If I keep very still everything will be all right.

Put the picture back in the box, Annie. Close the lid. I look up and see the red picture still on the easel. If I drew Julia now it would be looking proud, lonely, puzzled. She was never at home in the world, the world was always disappointing her. She wanted to be the centre of someone's attention and never was, found everything must be shared. 'I hate sharing,' she often said, though she would share the biscuits Dukie gave her if I found her before she finished them. She would give me pieces of nut and apple, would divide the stolen sherry. But these were not her mother's love, they were scraps, unimportant. When she grew up did her expression grow a little sardonic, the expression of a woman who sees only illusion? Did the Julia who went to that last party wear such an expression, the Julia who was forty-five, childless, beginning to quarrel with her husband?

If I don't open the box again, if I don't try to remember, nothing will hurt.

'Stay quite still,' says Julia's voice. 'It's only a stitch. It'll go away.' Her arm lies lightly on my shoulders as I stoop, not breathing. Her soap-and-clean-air Julia smell comes to me. 'Just wait a bit,' she says. 'Just wait.'

'Been busy?' David is ebullient, falsely cheerful. He is still in Germany and is not enjoying himself. He says Cologne is all right, the hotel is excellent, but he needs more shirts and he has indigestion. He thinks the widow has been tranquillized, having been sounding off all day to police, magistrates, anybody who would listen.

'Is she in your hotel?' I ask.

'Not grand enough, thank God. She travels in more style.' He would have knocked her out himself by eleven this morning if he hadn't decided to remain the polite English gentleman.

'You're not in trouble?' I can hear him breathing and it unnerves me. I have a premonition of bad news.

'I hope not. I think they're making a silly mistake. I don't think Buckley was mixed up in anything. He was shot by mistake. He was just unlucky. But the widow ...'

'Poor woman. Did she identify him?'

'... and the son wears dark glasses inside and out. Skinny ones. He looks ridiculous and sinister at the same time.'

A pause. 'Are you all right?' I demand.

He considers. He is an honest man. 'I would be if I could get out and do some sightseeing. See the ordinary world again.'

'Why not ask? They might be only too glad to show you around.'

'The police?'

'Why not?'

'I think you're being over-optimistic,' says David.

*

99

Sam says this girl he knows is going to Arizona to work on a ranch, showing greenhorns how to rope cattle. There's to be a party, a big send-off. He won't be home tonight.

'Does she know how to rope cattle?' I am stooped over a recipe book but am coming to realise we have none of the ingredients – for anything – in the house.

'No idea, I don't think. But the ranch people are supposed to teach her, then she teaches the guests.'

This sort of opportunity passed me by when I was young. Or maybe didn't actually exist. I could have helped on a kibbutz or dug wells in Ethiopia or taught African women the basic hygiene of a Western lifestyle. Worthy occupations, no doubt. Or seen as such by people with no imaginations and rather too much missionary zeal. I don't remember anyone suggesting ranches in Arizona.

'I wouldn't mind a send-off,' breathes Gina, who has long desired escape to South America.

'Your turn will come,' says Sam eagerly.

'I can't do any of these,' I confess, closing the book.

'Probably as well,' says Sam.

The phone goes.

'Wim,' says Gina, holding it out. 'He sounds cross.'

But he is not cross, simply businesslike. Have I no pictures for him at all? He hints that he is finding me increasingly unreliable, temperamental even.

'I'm working every day,' I tell him.

'But what are you producing?'

'Everybody goes through bad patches.'

'It's to do with France ...'

'Of course not.'

'What happened in France, Annie?'

The following day I visit the piano child. I find her

flushed, almost distressed. She has only just come in from school and needs time to adjust. For a moment I see an ordinary little girl, overheated by the scrum on the school bus. All afternoon she has been adding and subtracting or labelling a diagram of the eye. Little Miss Stiffneck, concert pianist, is temporarily somewhere else.

'Do I have to?' she asks, but not plaintively. She knows she has to, her father is standing there with that grim down-to-business look. He is a small man and he moves quietly but I find him threatening. The mother, a large, blowsy, ineffectual woman, wanders in and out offering me tea or gin or something to eat. I say no thank you politely on several occasions, but still she comes back, anxious, hesitant, confused as to her role and my requirements. Or perhaps she is simply giving the child time to recover, time to put on the armour.

Eventually Claire sits at the piano. She has put on the best dress, the armour. The small face is pale and stiff. No expression in the eyes. 'Do you want me to play anything?' she asks when her father leaves the room at my request. He is reluctant to go, returns almost at once on some trifling excuse. I tell him that if he doesn't go I shall have to, I can't concentrate. He is obviously not used to being told things like this. He hovers, then departs.

'No, just sit there a moment. What happened at school today?'

'Nothing. Bor-ring.' There is a flicker there. Chinks in the armour then.

'I wasn't much good at school.' This isn't strictly true but I can fib in a good cause. My mother taught me most of what I remember though, and a girl called Sis helped me through the darker reaches of geometry, and Julia – who had a court at Charleshall, of course –

101

taught me the solid backhand that won the house tennis trophy.

'Did you play netball?' She can't really believe I was ever a child.

'Yes, but badly. I was short. And worse, short-sighted.'

The father comes back in to see why we're talking. He thinks artists sketch in silence, or if they don't, ought to. I pack everything up at once and say that if he wants me to finish the portrait he'll have to bring the child to the studio and leave her there. Perhaps he doesn't want me to finish it? I repeat this. He goes deeply red and, for the moment, is lost for a suitable reply.

As I make my way to the front door he follows with the grimness of a man who never capitulates. Especially to artists who are bloody-minded, capricious and surplus to the requirements of modern civilisation. Only he does want a portrait of the child at the piano and I have been recommended, someone has told him I've tackled a mayor or two, some old county landowners, a couple of actors, a footballer, not to speak of the cellist, that other prodigy. I am a nuisance but he had decided to put up with me. Can he capitulate then without seeming to? He must. If I leave like this I might mention to someone he's an interfering old nanny.

I say goodbye to the wife. She's flustered. Have I finished already? No, but I can't stand being spied on. There has to be a rapport between artist and sitter, of some kind, of any kind. How can I achieve it in this house? I'm sure they'll find another painter. There are plenty of portraitists, though not all are very good.

'You're back early,' says Sam. He has put on some spaghetti for Gina and himself and has made a sauce, very creditable, but this waiting for the moment, for *al dente perfetto*, is too nerve-racking. His hair has crinkled in the steam from bending over the pan.

'I resigned.'

'You've never done that before,' remarks Gina. She looks at me with awe, her bold, intemperate mother. I've sometimes talked of pouring boiling oil over certain clients but have never done it yet.

'That wretched child . . . ' I begin.

'He might double the price if only you'll finish it.' Sam is the optimist.

'But it's not just about price.'

At this point the phone rings and it is, naturally, the father hoping I will do the picture. He is certainly not humble and he speaks with an unfortunate nasal twang as if he's trying to blow his nose, or is holding it because artists are stinking, irrational and subhuman.

'You didn't give in?' Gina accuses.

'He's bringing her over on Saturday.'

'Oh Ma, how could you?'

'I could because it's an all-right picture, maybe a good picture. I want to do it.'

They look at me across the table, across the spaghetti I have not, with motherly affection, provided. They know I frequently become emotionally involved with the strangers who sit to me to my detriment and theirs. They look tolerant, even a little amused.

'You'll feel better when you've eaten,' says Sam with the brisk platitudinous tones of a grandparent.

When we drew up at St Vierge Judith was the first to get out. Of course. She got out and made for the door but before she reached it it opened and Arlette was there, a thin figure in an apron. She was holding something, a cloth, a duster. She gave a little shriek. She said something. She was smiling. Judith stepped inside. The door was pushed to, not quite closed, not open. You can come in if you like, it suggested, but no one will mind if you don't.

We climbed out, stood on the drive, uncertain. We were simply excess baggage. A woman, after all, has to escape how and when she can. She is frequently encumbered by children, sometimes by a husband. These things are worked round or over. She had to bring us, the dour Julia, the disaffected boys, solid little Annie, but we are to keep out of the way, to amuse ourselves ... elsewhere. She hopes we are going to have fun but she is not here to make sure we do.

She was in love. Everything but Alain was subsidiary, irrelevant.

I remember it was Georgie who led the way into the house. Julia did not come in for a long time and when she did, made no sound and remained in shadow, aware she was not wanted, that none of us was wanted.

The child is delivered as promised. Gina brings her to the studio. Away from home she looks more childlike but is hampered by the best bloody dress, the severely scraped-back hair. She is politely incurious, but when she thinks I'm safely occupied her eyes dart about. When, after three-quarters of an hour, Gina brings in coffee and doughnuts as instructed, she announces she isn't given such things usually and falls on them in exemplary wolfish fashion. Gina gives me a startled look. So what is she fed on, bread and water? There are bits of sugar and a smear of jam on the best dress. 'I've got to play the piano all afternoon,' she remarks at some point when her mouth is less full. 'I hate Saturdays.'

To amuse her I take her to the summerhouse. Children like small secret places. Some of us never grow out of it. The building is nearly hidden now, a wayfaring tree, a laburnum, the young beech dipping and swaying about it. And the swans are there on the river, moving slowly away towards the bridge.

'I wish *I* had a boat,' says Claire.

She sits on the bank under the willow and for a moment is quite ordinary, with the vague greedy secret expression of childhood. Her hair is not simply black, the sun strikes a scarlet from the depths. She hates the dress but for the minute has forgotten it, does not care if she stains it with grass and river mud. Shortly the dread father will arrive to whisk her away to piano and purgatory.

'You can come again,' I say, though there is no reason why she should. 'You can row the boat.'

When she has gone I put up the canvas again and begin. It is absorbing but difficult. What I have achieved so far strikes me as clumsy. I want to do her justice. Try again, Annie. On the other hand, I know what I'm being paid for; the age-old dilemma, please oneself or please one's patron. There's no dodging the fact: the patron pays. Or does not if one plays silly buggers.

So. Here are the hands which were blobs becoming real hands on real piano keys. They are hesitant though. After all they are not sure. Sometimes the power in the music frightens her. And she knows she has become a slave to these keys which have already subtly shaped her fingers, to all those scales, to allegro assai, to arpeggios, sonatas. To all the paraphernalia. The face resolves itself too. Still unfinished but ... Here is the character pushing through the pigment. She is grave, defensive, the underlip pushed up a little. Why are you staring? Well, stare then, I didn't care. A baby still under the skin, under this pale, rapidly toughening skin of the reluctant prodigy. And yes, look, clever old Annie, all those foxy tones in the black black hair.

Gina is down the garden. I spot her through the geraniums. She too dislikes Saturdays. Longed for all week, they are invariably an anticlimax. She ought to be doing homework, can't be bothered, wanders about aimlessly. She sees me looking out and waves. Can I see her? Have I got my specs on? When I wave back she approaches, warier than the cat, knowing the studio is sacred ground. But I unlock the glass door and let her inside. She shivers.

'I thought it would be really warm in the sun.' Then her eyes slide away to the easel. 'Poor kid.'

'Well?'

She stares, squints, steps back and forth. 'I think it's her. I don't know. She looked a gloomy kid to me. And that horrible dress. I like the angle of the piano. It almost makes it seem more important than the figure, but not quite. That was clever.'

'It just happened.'

And I see what I am painting suddenly, the tyranny of talent, of the exaggerated expectations of those we love. But then again it is just a child at a piano about to try the opening bars of something difficult and not looking forward to it, her teacher has a fine line in sarcasm and her father dislikes failure too, does not allow for the necessary struggle.

'Can we eat?' asks Gina.

'He won't pay for it,' I say, nodding at the picture.

'He will if he's any sense. Anyway, Wim will buy it. Or sell it for you.'

'I feel tired.' And I do. I drag off the elastic band and let my hair frizz out above my shoulders. You should have it cut, Annie, have it coloured. Can't be bothered. Anyway, if I had it cut where would I stick my brushes when I need my hands free? Tell me that. A bird's nest comes in useful.

Gina puts an arm through mine. Cosy. Suspicious.

106

'Can we eat?' she asks again.

I ring the hotel in Cologne.

'Herr Somerville is out,' says reception. A cool young man, excellent English naturally, sorry he cannot help. Do I want to leave a message?

I leave a message.

Saturday. Police work every day, don't they? Should I be worried? For all I know David is just out on the town at last, walking about, lingering in cafés, looking into churches, not listening to guides. He hates guides, likes to be among people going about their ordinary business. He is bored by ruins and palaces and folk dancing. I imagine him finding a market, trying out his barking German and being pleased when people understand.

David, where are you?

I am not satisfied with young Claire. I am not satisfied with the piano.

I don't know why I painted over Julia.

I ring Cologne again but there is still no David.

In bed at night I turn on the light to read because I can't sleep and I see the box, Julia's box, on the chest of drawers. The children have already forgotten all about it, it has proved such a disappointment. If I put it away in the cupboard even David will fail to nag me about it, he will be too full of this business in Cologne.

And that will be that, Ju.

At Charleshall I hid in the yew hedges and the box hedges and in the branches of trees and behind cold frames and under shelving in the glasshouses. I hid in the tool sheds, the stables, or far down the long drive by the rusting iron gates that were shut. Sometimes Julia found me, sometimes not. Often I grew tired of waiting and emerged, ran about, dared Fate to send her round the corner, over the gravel, at that very minute. It was a disappointment, trudging back to the house, giving up because she had not come. When it was her turn to hide things were no better, I could never be sure she was there. Now and then I lost my temper, hurtled down the paths, charged through the stable yard. 'Juliaaaa ...' I would yell, arms outstretched, head thrown back. 'Juliaaa ...'

Now I know where she is hiding I do not want to find her.

I turn out the light abruptly and the box vanishes.

Chapter Ten

I thought, waking to the sound of Sunday bells, that everything was in place, predictable. But the bells had no sooner stopped than the phone rang, twice, and each time the day took on a darker tone.

David, husky and anxious, rings from the hotel. 'They think he was shot by a Frenchman.'

'How do they know?'

'The woman downstairs.'

'She can recognise a Frenchman on a dark landing?'

'He spoke to her. Asked her for the flat.'

'But whose flat was it? Why was Buckley there?'

'A man called Brinkmann. An accountant. No one has any idea why Buckley went to see him or how he came to die in the living room when Brinkmann was out. How did he get in?'

'Brinkmann gave him a key.'

'He says not. He also says there had been no arrangement to meet. He says he knew Buckley only very slightly through their mutual dealings with a small engineering company lately taken over by some set-up in Hamburg. He has an alibi and no record of getting into trouble.'

'And the mysterious Frenchman? Did he speak French then?'

'I doubt it. But the woman's convinced. French, she

109

says.' Thus buggering up international relations even further.

'But what's it to do with you? Why do you have to be there?'

'They're trying to build a profile, understand how he operated. Fraud, smuggling, lots of things they're not talking about. It's taking them a while to accept the innocent country solicitor at face value. But I'll be home tomorrow. Just one more chat with the young inspector at the end of the corridor.' He draws in a long breath, contemplating this. 'You know, I've had to buy clothes and razor blades and even handkerchiefs,' he adds mournfully.

'You needed some anyway.' What is the difference between buying hankies in Colchester or Cologne?

'Look, can you ring Bibs, reassure her.'

'About what?'

'That I'm still around, I suppose. I've sent about a hundred faxes to Will but nothing's come back.'

'He's probably ignoring them, quite sensibly.'

'You don't understand. Just ring Bibs.' Something else occurs to him. 'Are you painting?'

'Of course I'm painting.'

'The piano child?'

'The piano child.'

He rings off quite cheerily, now he can put down wifely ill-humour to the hormonal disruptions of artistic endeavour. Poor thing, she can't help it. And besides, after tomorrow he will no longer have to wrestle with all these great long uvula-destroying German nouns.

'Was that Daddy? Is he coming home?' asks Gina, appearing in the doorway. I nod yes and yes. Her face clears. She is wearing some old pyjamas of Sam's which are too big. She has rolled the arms and legs up so that she can walk safely with the tray of tea she is bearing proudly towards the bed.

'A treat,' she says.

Then Wim. He is in a place called Oldenzaal. His car has broken down. Modern cars shouldn't do this, especially expensive Swedish ones. He is incensed. Hanging about, he has had time to think. What is it I'm working on? A child? What sort of child, what sort of picture, what size? Whatever I say he sounds dissatisfied, asks more questions. I tell him I've done a few landscapes. This is pure spite. I know exactly what he will say.

'Playing about. You're a painter of people, not trees and fields. So have they any people in them, these landscapes?'

I explain I find landscapes restful just because there are no people. Wim says it's a question of involvement. He says he knows I struggle with faces, bleed to do them justice. Hard work, yes, but what I should be doing all the time. Landscapes, pooh – only he doesn't say pooh, he says some Dutch word I thankfully miss – water and cows, a lot of green and grey.

'Aelbert Cuyp,' I murmur.

The line crackles. 'Damn Cuyp,' says Wim. He's trying to launch an exhibition of contemporary women artists but there's resistance in all but the smallest galleries. He isn't going to be put off though. He wants some strong stuff to make an impact.

'I want faces,' he says, 'not pretty views.'

'Turner didn't paint pretty views,' I tell him.

The line crackles again. There is a blast of foreign hubbub.

'The car is ready. Are you there, Annie? I want something inspired. O.K.? Inspired, Annie. The best.'

'Where on earth is Oldenzaal?' I ask.

*

111

I go for a walk round the town. David and Wim have upset me. I don't know why. The sun is watery and fitful, the pavements damp. People are not up yet or are eating a late breakfast. I walk in a purposeful way as if on a hike with compass and iron rations, distant peaks beckoning. In a shop window I catch a glimpse of this eccentric figure with wild hair clumping along in wellingtons. The jumper I have borrowed from Sam has an exploding heart on the front. But artists can be forgiven for appearing in public like this, everyone knows they are all slightly mad.

I pass the Lamb and Flag, the King's Head, the market cross, swing left-handed back down to the river. I smell coffee and toast, wood smoke, pear blossom. Plunging down the steps to the little foot-bridge by the sawmill I find a solitary fisherman baiting his line. The water seems dank here, full of weed. Ash and alder grow thick and keep out the sun. I hurry across to the marshes where the cattle are all lying down and the larks are singing. My homely Cuyp.

'It's a good thing I saw you from the bathroom,' says Sam. He has rowed over to rescue me from the far bank. I hoped someone would see me, jumping up and down and waving my arms, otherwise it meant a quarter-mile trek to the bridge and back along the road.

'I had to get out, get some fresh air.'

'I thought you were having some sort of fit.'

'I couldn't bear it, the boat moored twenty feet away and no way of getting across.'

'You'd better not make a habit of it. You'll frighten the neighbours.'

We bump the bank under the willow. Stepping out and making fast I see the swans floating serenely towards the bridge.

'Shouldn't one of them be sitting on the eggs?' asks
Sam.

Sam is going out again. A different girl.
'I can't think what they see in him,' says Gina
disdainfully.
'He's not bad-looking,' I suggest.
'You always say women want more than that.'
Do I? 'I hope they do.'
'Well then.'

Alain was certainly not handsome. Rather he had a
face pieced together, seams of experience, laughter,
concentration. Interesting, a woman might say. Nice
bones, big and flat, and a general air of kindliness,
dependability. A good doctor probably, one who
would listen.
He wanted to know my name.
'Annie, isn't it? Julia's friend Annie. Such fiery
hair. Beautiful.' He sounded as if he meant it.
He sat on the terrace under the mulberry, smoking.
We were alone. Why? I can't remember. Judith and
Arlette might have gone to the village, to market. The
boys might have been in the ravine, climbing trees,
shooting arrows. Julia was at the farm, fetching the
milk. She liked doing this, she could be a long time
and make Judith worry.
'And how do you like France, Annie?'
I told him about Rouen, Béthune, Laon, Coutances.
'You've got about,' he said, amused. He thought my
mother was brave, taking to the road in an old car and
with two small children. Not so small now, of course.
He understood my rather treacherous description of
Tottie. His own sister had screamed for two years, he
said, his mother had nearly tossed her off the mountain. Then one day she had stopped, had become

113

cheerful and sunny, so much so that she was known –
or had been, she was a mother herself by this time – as
little peach. We laughed over this.

I don't know how long we sat. Minutes, half an
hour. The blue smoke of his cigarette wreathed among
the mulberry leaves. He was dressed casually as if he
had been gardening or mending a car. He did not seem
like a doctor. His accent was impeccable, upper class.
He said his grandmother had run away from the
château to marry his grandfather, a poor research
student, and brought her children up like milords in
spite of having no money. His father, also a doctor,
had tried to mend the family rift but had failed. And
now the old house was empty, everyone dead or far
away.

I didn't have a father, I told him. My mother taught
music and let out part of the house. This year we had a
Greek student and a shy grey-haired mathematician
from Harvard on some kind of exchange.

'And does your mother have red hair?'

'Not as red as mine.'

More contemplation of the mulberry leaves. 'And
where is Julia this morning?'

'Gone for the milk.' I felt an explanation was
needed. 'I'm here to look after Tim and Georgie.'

No one had said so. No one had given me this
charge. But Julia had not wanted me with her at the
farm. These days she was grumpy, spiteful, hardly
speaking.

'Julia is not like her mother,' Alain said quietly.

'No.' It had never occurred to me she ought to be.
'Not to look at.' Or in any other way.

'Like Monsieur perhaps?'

'The Major?' I shook my head. Julia seemed only
like Julia.

'And this house, St Vierge. Do you like it?'

'I could stay for ever,' I said quite truthfully.

It comes back to me: the warm stones beneath my fingers, the sun on my shoulders, the big hands holding the cigarette, the way his hair sprang dark and dusty as if he were a boy who'd been climbing trees. He was lying back in Judith's chair, relaxed, smiling.

He spoke of Judith eventually. Did I like her? Didn't I think she was kind? A kind, lovely woman, rather sad. Like a lost child. No, I wanted to say, that's Julia. But I didn't speak. He didn't need me to, only to listen. Yes, Annie, a lost child. One believes people must be happy but it turns out otherwise. *On croit ... On croit* but nothing is certain. And a woman like Judith is entitled to love.

All this into my head and over it. He was suffering from conscience perhaps. When he paused he would light another cigarette from the stub of the last. Doctors know what's best but never do it, he told me, laughing.

Then the noise of the car, Arlette's shrill demanding call. A door opened and closed. 'But where are the children, oh God not in the river,' exclaimed Judith on one breath, hurrying on to the terrace.

'*Bonjour*. See, I was early. Why the panic? Annie and I have been talking. I think the boys are in the woodshed being wounded soldiers.' He rose, stooped to kiss her on each cheek. Then another, on the bridge of her nose, because they were alone, who was there to see? Only Annie. Annie didn't count.

Then they were really alone. Annie was running down to the *bassin*. She's gone without her hat again, Judith would have said.

And I forgot all this for thirty years.

Why should I remember it now, mixing my colours for the piano child? I haven't opened the box. I am looking forward to this luminous indigo on my brush,

115

not thinking of France, of Alain, of the smell of herbs, of the cool water in the *bassin* breaking under my hands.

Paint, Annie. Just paint.

I lodge the brush in my hair. The house is very quiet. I go upstairs and sit in the chair by the window with the box on my knees.

Hello, Julia.

Judith was on the terrace. She had been in the small garden at the side of the house where the vegetables are grown. A basket of beans and lettuce and parsley stood under her chair. She sat with her feet on the wall. Her legs were bare, smooth and brown. She had nice feet, well-tended. I realised I had never seen my mother's feet, they were always in sensible shoes slopping through English downpours, in boots, in satin evening shoes, the sort she wore for concerts. When was the last time we sat on a beach, paddled or swam?

'My mother would like it here,' I said.

'I expect she would. Does she ever get a holiday? Away from you two, I mean.'

'No.' The possibility of it had never crossed my mind.

I crouched on the stones watching the little lizards flicking in and out of holes in the wall. The sunlight was not so strong now, four o'clock, a golden, dusty time.

'Are you happy, Annie?' Her eyes were closed, her loose hair falling over the cushions.

'Yes.' The one word will do. I was happy.

Silence, except for the insects in the rosemary bushes, the imperceptible rustle of the lizards.

'Where's Julia?'

'She went to the farm,' I said.

116

'But it's so late. She's already been once today.'

'She likes it there. Monsieur Blanchard takes her to look at things.'

'What things?'

'Oh, goats, the chestnuts drying, his vat of wine.'

'Wine?'

She moved her legs abruptly, swung them down. Thinking of Julia always made her anxious. And I had noticed that one moment she could be the Judith of Charleshall, pale and vague – did these moments coincide with letters from the Major? – the next a glowing Judith, warm and golden as if recharged by the sun. When Alain came? He came nearly every evening, not always to eat. He was a busy man and snatched time when he could. But by now Arlette always laid another place, no longer expected his knock. He opened the door himself or walked round to the terrace. If it was late and the cool of the mountain air had driven us indoors he might stand out there looking in, as if it gave him pleasure just to see us in the lamplight; no electricity at St Vierge in those days. He would wait, smoking, patient, until Judith looked up and smiled.

That night, in bed, Julia said, 'That man's always here. It's all Mother cares about.' The springs creaked as she turned. 'She doesn't take any notice of anyone else.'

The boys don't want notice taken of them, they might be stopped from climbing so high, from playing down near the river. I have enough notice taken of me. And Arlette notices Julia, brushes her slippery hair every night, tells her she's growing pretty, soon the boys ... Monsieur Blanchard takes notice, explaining his machinery, leading her through his dusty barns.

'Oh, go to sleep,' I said.

I slept. And dreamt. A vague eroticism had invaded my dreams since coming to St Vierge. Sometimes I recognised Alain's face, his hands, his slow pleasant cultured voice. He did nothing spectacular or menacing, was, as in life, distantly affectionate, did not touch, only came close to instantly fade away among people I did not know. Always he was just there, there being Alain, but my body felt the lighter for it, floating on inexplicable happiness. I woke contented, like the cats in their straw hollows in the old goat house. For breakfast there was coffee and the tough salty bread and mulberry jelly and the goat cheese Arlette bought from her aunt in the little house up the track. Every morning I hurried downstairs while Julia stayed behind, the sheets over her head. She never spoke, pretended to be asleep.

'*Bonjour*, Mademoiselle Annie.'

'*Bonjour*, Arlette.'

But then Arlette told Judith Monsieur Blanchard had a reputation for touching up young girls. The younger the better, said Arlette. Twelve, thirteen, fourteen. Her voice was breathy and apologetic. She didn't like to use coarse expressions to Judith, who was a lady. She was rolling pastry and her hands were stilled, braced, in the floury mess on the old table. There were strands of hair stuck to her hot forehead. She blew them away with her bottom lip thrust out comically. 'Do you understand, Madame?' Of course, she added comfortingly after a moment, it might be nothing ...

I was outside in the passage. I stood perfectly still, unable to go in or go back. They hadn't heard me coming but they would be sure to hear me retreat. It would seem as if I eavesdropped. Life can be like that, casting the innocent into such traps. I stood, barefoot on the stone floor, pressed up against the wall.

'Oh surely ...' Judith began. Arlette was not wholly to be trusted.

'It's just that she's there so much.'

'But Madame Blanchard is there.'

'In the house.' And then, with a shrug, 'Perhaps.'

'Oh, nonsense!' cried Judith robustly.

'But Madame ...'

'Well, all right. I'll tell her she can't go again by herself.' Judith did not have her heart in motherhood but she knew lines must be drawn. All the same, should she take any of it seriously? Arlette was such a gossip.

But what was it Monsieur Blanchard did, I wondered.

'He's harmless enough probably.' Arlette had begun on the pastry again, working in butter with deft fingers. 'Just a dirty old man. Send Annie with her.'

'I don't know.'

'But yes, Madame. Let Annie go. She's a good girl. If he tried anything on she'd spit in his eye.'

There was a pause.

'What would her mother say?' said Judith.

My mother would have said fetch the milk Annie, you know how to look after yourself. So I did, leaving Julia in a sulk, walking on up through the trees swinging my milk can. A long way away I could hear the old woman calling her goats, a high-pitched whooping noise. Arlette was embarrassed by her, told us she was mad, she kept her money in her mattress and in winter had the goats in by the fire. I thought this sensible. My only objection to her was the smell of goat that clung to everything about her. Now if she had smelt of cows ...

There was the smell of cow in the Blanchards' yard, and of poultry and sun-warmed earth. The house was very old, much larger than St Vierge, half of it shut off. 'Well, there are only the two of us now,' Monsieur had once told me. There had been three children. The daughters had married and lived far away, the son had died at fourteen. He had had an ear infection. Why should someone die of an ear infection? What did Monsieur do or want to do in the dark corners between the wine vats? He had always taken pains to keep his oily overalls away from my clean clothes, had seemed ordinary and cheerful, had gladly repeated whatever I had misunderstood. I rather liked him.

Today Madame, a bloated, amiable woman, trusted me with a basket of eggs as well as the milk. She made me coffee and cut me some cakey stuff, a sort of brioche. She didn't ask after Julia but after Judith, the beautiful Madame Hawsley – which she pronounced Oselee – and after Arlette, such a good cook, such pastry. When Monsieur came in he said, 'Well, we don't see much of you. Only Mademoiselle Julia.' But he didn't sound disappointed that she hadn't come. He asked if we were the same age. I said yes. 'Everyone is different, eh?' was what I thought he said then. He was looking at Madame over my head. 'Like our girls. Remember?' But there was a lot more, unspoken, in the look.

'Look what I've brought,' I said to Arlette.

She picked one out, turned it reverently in her hand, a great brown speckled egg, a masterpiece. The hen should have a medal for it, she exclaimed. I loved the way she did this, made everyday things so special.

Being French she added, 'Omelettes perhaps tonight?' and winked.

Alain and Judith were on the terrace looking at a book. They were laughing. Low, intimate, intensely private laughter. I hesitated but they had heard me, glanced up. I was an intrusion but not an unwelcome one. They were so happy. They smiled and Judith held out a hand.

'They gave me some eggs,' I said. 'At the farm. Because they liked you, I think.' Her hand was warm and dry, very thin.

'How sweet. Tell me, are you going to wear your hair in that plait for ever and ever? It makes you look so young.'

'But she is young,' said Alain. 'And she won't appreciate being teased. Who can blame her?'

'But she has such lovely red hair.'

He detached my hand from hers, took it in his own. 'Annie, how would you like to visit Avignon?'

It was just a name to me. I smiled hopefully, as children do, unsure what was expected.

'You'll like it there,' Judith assured me. 'You and Julia.'

'I bet you let him kiss you behind the wine vats,' I said. 'An old man like that. How could you?'

But Julia was too angry, or too wise, to reply.

Of course she wouldn't come to Avignon.

'Playing gooseberry,' she said. 'Just so they can look respectable.'

I didn't understand. I thought she was simply determined to spoil a happy day. She had spent all this holiday in killjoy mood, fractious and perverse. I remember Judith talked to her alone before we went to bed that night but nothing came of it. 'I won't go,' said Julia, and was too big to coerce, always at the limits of Judith's control. 'I won't go.' I heard the words spoken with the finality I recognised. After this, one would plead in vain. It was as if the essential Julia withdrew behind a barricade, leaving an automaton. Such stubbornness was inhuman, it was so emotionless, her face quite still, her eyes blank. It was when she grew cold like this I had learned to leave her, to go

121

off about the garden alone, to join the cousins, to seek out Dukie, to play with Judith's little dog.

'I won't go,' said Julia.

'But darling . . . ' said Judith.

And so of course she did not come, and I went with Judith and Alain to Avignon and it was hot and tiring and exciting, and we stayed the night in a small *pension* where I slept alone in a room with two beds. Every time I looked at the empty one it was as if Julia reproached me. But I didn't understand her reproaches. I was enjoying myself. I had not been made to feel a gooseberry. I had eaten dinner, drunk a little wine, talked, felt accepted for the first time in a wholly adult world.

'Your mother has always fascinated me,' said Judith. 'I would never have the courage to manage alone. And a baby coming at the worst time.'

I had never thought to question Tottie's arrival but she had, indeed, been inconvenient. And noisy.

'The baby was probably a godsend,' remarked Alain. He was lighting a small cigar.

'I suppose for some women babies are,' and then, glancing away across the other tables with their check cloths and their vociferous diners, 'life is so much easier when nature arranges the priorities. It's making choices that wears us down, and then wondering if they were the right ones.' After a little, as if her thoughts were fixed on babies, 'I was never much good with children.'

Lying in bed I wondered at Julia being Judith's daughter. It was as if I saw with unexpected clarity, no longer a child, permitted at last to ask and receive sensible answers. The sensible answer about Julia was surely that she was the Major's daughter, self-contained, uncommunicative, frequently morose. He took his pleasures seriously, Dukie had once said. Mystified, still I understood that he rarely laughed. Julia laughed but in between seemed to find the world too much for her, behaved oddly and inconsistently, then withdrew.

At St Vierge, when we returned, I found her in withdrawal.

'What do you think my father would say?'

'About what?'

'You are *so* stupid.'

I let her go. There was no point in my being passionate, demanding explanations. Besides, perhaps I knew all the answers already, but in my bones, and preferred to leave them there. It seemed to me, even then, that happiness was a too rare commodity and surely ought to be cherished.

But I did shout, running out of the bedroom and hanging over the stairs.

I shouted, 'You don't deserve to have any friends.'

'Annie? Is that you?'

'Who else?' All afternoon, on and off, I've been rooting in the box. I've been in the Cevennes under the mulberry. I've been hearing Alain's voice, seeing Judith's rueful look across the restaurant. 'I was never much good with children.' And I am breathless and disturbed like someone waking from a dream where something terrible threatens but never occurs.

'Are you all right?'

'I think so. How's Cologne?'

'I'm coming home tomorrow morning. Can you meet me?'

He passes on information about planes. I think, damn, I'll never get on with the piano child.

'Everything sorted out?'

'Hard to say. Anyway, I'm not wanted any more. The whole thing's a bloody muddle if you ask me. How's Gina?'

I tell him. He sounds reassured. He is glad we are cosily domestic, imagines us in unlikely harmony round the supper table talking over the day's events.

'Done any work?' he asks bouncily.

'Yes,' I lie.

Then I go to bed and read, and then pad barefoot down to the studio and turn on all the lights and stare at the piano child. The piano child is squinting crossly. Nothing is the right distance, the right tone, the right proportion. The piano is definitely too prominent, the child malevolent, and all the colours garish.

Dear God.

I open a bottle of wine and drink one glass and fall asleep in a kitchen chair.

I sleep twenty minutes and wake feeling like an old woman, aching in every joint. It is the arthritis of disappointment. I'm no good. I can't paint. Perhaps I make a passable mother, perhaps not. Even that is compromised by a tendency to half-heartedness, just as I am no more than a half-hearted wife and cook and house-cleaner.

'Darling.' Gina's light is still on and I burst in full of indignation. 'It's past midnight.'

'I know.' She is sitting up in bed apparently reading about the Weimar Republic.

'Was that Dad earlier? Is he all right?' She is increasingly worried about him. He is a big man having to tread softly across bogs. 'They won't arrest him?'

'What for? He'll be home tomorrow. Isn't it rather late for homework?'

'I've got a test. But I don't really understand any of it. What were they all doing?'

'I don't know. I think my history stopped at Waterloo.'

'That doesn't mean you don't know.'

'I suppose not. May we discuss it at breakfast? I want to go to bed.'

She sinks back on the pillows, a serene little face, rather beautiful. She is a Master of Flémalle madonna just before the angel speaks, minding her own girlish business, irreproachably pure and virtuous. Real life, cruel life, is still outside the door over there, the door that leads in all the pictures to the little formal garden, the river, the far off adventuring ships.

'Have you been in the box?' she asks.

'I don't know what I'm supposed to do with the stuff.'

'You must keep it.'

'What for? A lot of old letters, photos, even school reports.'

'It's history,' says Gina. Her face puckers for a kiss. 'Well, isn't it?' She looks as if, in a moment, she'll begin a serious talk on primary sources. Modern education is a fearsome thing.

I kiss her. She smells of spot cream and toothpaste.

'Don't forget,' she says. 'Breakfast. Weimar Republic.'

I turn out her light.

Chapter Eleven

It's history. You're history, Julia. And there is nothing of then in the now, and this moment, drawing the brush through the yielding paint, watching the light revealed and revealing. The girl's face tips forward out of shadow but the still-dark hollows of the eyes are watchful, proud and frightened. There is still this and this to do but otherwise ... No, it isn't as bad as I thought last night, frightening myself silly. I shall finish it today and next week will see if Daddy piano wants to pay for it. Who knows? I will either be showing him something he recognises but chooses to ignore, in which case goodbye, Annie, and take the picture with you, or ... Or he'll think it unusual, that unexpected angle for instance, but artists can't be trusted to see anything straight like ordinary mortals. 'Yes, it will do very well over the fireplace. Dear Claire at ten when we were all just realising what a future she might have. All history now, of course. This week she plays in New York.'

At ten I clean the brushes. I have been at work since six. My back aches. I have emerald green down my front and white all over my hands because the tube split. Damn tube. I feel I have been climbing mountains, but it's time to fling on a jacket and grab the car keys and roar away to the airport.

'I'm so sorry,' says the girl behind the desk. I find I am standing on tiptoe because the desk is high and I am both short and overwrought. The plane is late. There is thick fog over Holland. They estimate arrival in half an hour but this is just a lollipop to keep the children happy, especially this importunate child smelling of turps.

When I go to the Ladies I see I have Chinese white all over my nose.

For an hour I prowl about aimlessly until the plane drops down through the drizzle and lands in a series of ungainly jerks. There is an expanse of wet tarmac, very little going on, every horizon blanketed in mist. We could all be extras in a sixties film about the cold war. A double agent is expected. I hang about waiting for him in my grass-stained jacket, my shabby moccasins, my Chinese white nose. When David appears he is walking very slowly like an old man and looks totally exhausted. He is wearing a new shirt and a new tie and, quite possibly, new trousers. He also has a suitcase as well as the overnight bag. He sees me from a long way off and waves languidly as if the effort is almost too such. When he gets close enough he says, 'Did you know you've paint all over your face?' and then, in the same breath, 'If I don't have a decent cup of coffee soon I'll throw a tantrum.'

So we sit. He stirs sugar into his drink slowly, round and round. He never has sugar. We leave conversation aside for a while. He grunts and sighs.

'Everything O.K.?' he says at last. 'How's Gina?'

'You asked last night. She's fine.'

'And Will?'

'Bibs took him in hand. Even the baby's been sleeping through the night.'

'And you?' He is waking from the trance.

'I'm a brushstroke from finishing the piano child.'

We are half-way to the car when he puts down the bags and takes me in his arms. He is rarely demonstrative in public. But then this is a wide open, almost deserted expanse of parking bays.

'Is everything sorted? In Cologne.'

'I hope so,' he says, meaning not really.

'And did you get to see the town?'

'For an hour or two. I went there as a boy, did I tell you? Some of it's still the same.'

'Good for Cologne.' But I think suddenly of St Vierge. Some of it the same. That peculiar sweet dry smell under the oaks, for instance, and the sound of the river.

'You're shivering,' says David and keeps a protective arm about my shoulders. 'Why didn't you put on a coat?'

In the car he goes to sleep mid-sentence somewhere on the Norwich ring road.

I have put up a fresh canvas. Nothing so daunting as a fresh canvas. I have my apron on and my messy palette and my best palette and my fifty brushes and lots of old rags are lying ready, and I'm standing looking out at the garden, daunted. I see green, brown thatch between leaves, the cat stalking.

Where are you, Julia?

I turn round and begin to draw.

In the box is a slender little bracelet, silver wire and pearls, not expensive, a trinket. It is so fine it curls to nothing in the hollow of my palm. Judith bought it for me in Avignon. I had forgotten it. In all the disorder, the strangeness, the hurry of those last two days I must have left it by the bed, on the chest of drawers, or dropped on the floor. Did I miss it? Perhaps. Did I remember it afterwards? Perhaps. But now I hold it in

128

my hand again and remember everything.

When we got back there was a letter from the Major. It lay waiting on the oak chest in the passage. Judith stopped, picked it up, put it down. 'Hello, Arlette. So hot. Is there lemonade?' And Arlette brought lemonade to the shade of the mulberry and talked of the special dish she had made for our home-coming, delicate quenelles, a whole afternoon's preparation had gone into them. And then the boys running up, wanting presents, gabbling their adventures in the woods. And Julia, aloof and expressionless, taking in her hand the twin of my bracelet but with blue stones. She cared nothing for jewellery, nothing for any possessions, except her bear, except the rocking horse.

'Thank you,' she said primly.

But a minute later she had gone and the bracelet lay abandoned on the table.

'Never mind,' said Judith.

'Julia, why not go and swim?' Judith asked. Is this the next morning? Possibly. She was reading a book under the mulberry. There was a bowl of coffee on the table next to her. The bowl was pale blue, big as a soup dish. Inside was a small insect swimming gamely for his life.

'She thinks there are snakes,' I told her. I was sitting at her feet, poking a stick into the cracks in the wall hoping to disturb the lizards.

'Don't be silly. Arlette says it's quite safe. Anyway,' tartly, 'Annie and the boys are always swimming there.'

'I don't care anything about snakes. I just don't want to swim. It doesn't matter to me what Annie does,' Julia said.

For Julia, this is an outburst. Judith stirs, alert to

change. All this holiday Julia has retreated into silence, into the dim upstairs of the house, into far reaches of the woods, into Monsieur Blanchard's barns. We have given up trying to coax, placate or understand.

'I'm going to the farm,' Julia announced.

Judith was bending over the coffee trying to rescue the insect. Triumphantly she spooned it out and watched it drying in the sunshine by her saucer.

'Not without Annie,' she said calmly. There was a new calm about her that day. It was somehow connected to her obvious happiness, to Alain, to Avignon. It was not the vague, uninterested calm of Charleshall where she passed from room to garden and back like a ghost.

'I don't want to go with Annie.' Julia didn't look at me.

'Then you'll stay here.'

'Why?'

'Listen,' said Judith. 'You're not a child any more. I explained why the other evening.'

But not to me, I thought rather crossly. Why wasn't there any warning for me?

'He's all right,' Julia protested. 'He doesn't do anything.' She meant: I'm going, I don't care.

'Julia.' A warning note. A mother's voice. Judith was so seldom like a mother, hard-edged, peremptory, protective.

Julia's face was still expressionless. After a moment she went into the house.

Judith sighed and picked up her book.

I poked my stick at the lizards.

The insect flew away.

Here we are in a school photo. Julia is next to me though they must have tried to separate us; she is so much taller, she belonged in the back row with the biggies. At some moment of confusion she must have squeezed through or crawled under so that we were together again. Her hair looks shiny in the sun, a neat bob. I sport the usual pigtail that drops, carroty, over one shoulder. Julia has a bust, I have none. Julia has poise, I am just standing there hoping it will soon be over and we can go home early.

A hundred children. In the front row the boys – boys attended till they were eight – sit arms folded. They all look remarkably tough. I remember they had their own part of the playground, practically their own language. We older girls don't even acknowledge their existence. We stand shoulder to shoulder, smothering giggles, squinting. Names come back to me: Susan, Caroline, Sis. Sis short for Cecilia. Her long good-natured face grins out. She doesn't mind the photographer, the fussing teachers, the fact that we are looking into the sun. If Julia had not been there Sis and I would have been best friends. After Julia it was too late. I felt in limbo, betrayed, unclaimed. Then came exams, girls leaving. We were moody and anxious, busy growing up. Sis left, went out to work. It was as if an anchor cable had parted. My mother worried. She understood. 'Why not keep in touch?' she said, meaning with Sis, whom she had always liked. But I never did. Nothing was quite in focus or properly in proportion. Sis was out in the world with a purpose and I was ... somewhere else. Somewhere.

My mother never quite forgave Julia those years of inexplicable silence.

'What happened to her, I wonder?' she said once during the long weeks when she was dying.

'I've never thought about it.' Julia? Who's she? 'Not for years anyway.'

'I felt so sorry for her mother. Such a nice woman.'

131

And so here is the photo of the inseparable friends before. Before whatever: circumstance, time, puberty, death had done their bit. On the back Julia has written in her crowded hand: second row, Annie and Julia.

This was the spring term before St Vierge.

'Whenever you look into that bloody box you come over all pale and pinched,' says David.

'I'm sorry.'

'What d'you mean, you're sorry? What is it about this Julia that makes you behave like this?'

'Just memories. You know.'

'No, I don't know. Not happy ones, I can tell that.'

'Some of them.'

'Not many.'

The canvas is no longer virgin. It is filled with the outline of Julia on the rocking horse.

Of course.

Of course Charleshall. Of course the rocking horse. Say Julia and that is where I see her, Charleshall. Dog leads in the back kitchen, carbolic smell, wellingtons in rows, the doors all standing open to the sun or firmly closed against rain and rough winds. At any time of the year you knew what to expect, vases of flowers, rice pudding, apple fritters, hot milk before bed. There was routine and ritual, Dukie in her kitchen, the Major about his woods and fields, the daily girls cycling away on the dot of one.

'It must take a lot of dusting,' my mother said of the house. She would have worried that the cellars were damp, the gutters leaked. She knew the burden of these things. 'You need money for a place like that,' she remarked after one of her brief visits to collect me. She could see money was in short supply. Children don't think of these things. The war, the Labour government, had struck the Hawsleys down. Only a few things remained, the Winterhalters, the ancient Turkey rugs, the Broadwood.

'Play it,' Judith said. 'I expect it's out of tune though it's regularly cosseted by the tuner. Go on. I mean it. I can't play a note and my husband isn't in the least musical. It was his mother's so has a rather dubious sentimental value.'

My mother, tempted, lifted the lid. A note. Another. Then, like a rider with the measure of the obstacle ahead, she began. Debussy perhaps. I have forgotten. I know the piano sounded quite different from the one we had at home, mellower, richer. It might have been an illusion. It might have been just the big room, the tall windows, the strange atmosphere of threadbare gentility. Judith, perched on the arm of a chair, was struck into profound stillness. In the hall outside the open door someone had stopped to listen – Dukie? – was holding her breath. I felt embarrassed, then suddenly pleased. My mother is playing for you, playing properly for you, I wanted to tell them. She played in Vienna and Paris once. Until now I had not understood. A career cut short, no money, a severe teacher limiting her public appearances, a broken arm. It was as if the world conspired against me, she had told me once. By the time the arm mended she had met my father. Until now I had accounted him sufficient compensation.

'How wonderful to play like that,' said Judith.

And my mother was very modest. It was a privilege, she said, to make music on such a lovely instrument.

So in stiff and formal phrases they disguised the fact that they had both been unbearably moved.

At Charleshall there were paper and paints for rainy days. In the day nursery there were tins of charcoal, lead pencils, chalks. Under the old textbooks on the

133

shelves were folders of Edwardian watercolours done by great-aunts on walking holidays. 'Oh, they all came from Sussex,' Julia would say airily. There had been some other Charleshall in Sussex where they had all grown up, the great-aunts, the grandparents, the Major himself. The Winterhalters, the piano, the rocking horse had come from there. 'Pulled down,' said Julia when I asked her what had happened. 'They built lots of new houses all over where it was.' And no money seemed to have come to the Hawsleys. I imagined them treading through the ruins retrieving their few heirlooms. I knew nothing of bank loans, mortgages, the gloomy rituals of insolvency.

'But where did all the great-aunts go?' I demanded on the long afternoons we were imprisoned with their drawings, their pressed flowers, their commonplace books and yellowed, fragile magazines.

'Good Heavens! They're all dead, poor old darlings,' said Judith. But she had seen I liked drawing. I had sketched all the dogs, had painstakingly copied a view of Cairo.

'That's all she does indoors,' said Julia scornfully. Scornful-affectionate. 'She draws.'

For my birthday that year the Hawsleys gave me a box of watercolours, professional artist watercolours. My mother didn't say My God, who in their right mind would buy such a thing for a ten year old? She was an artist herself. She only said, 'Take care of them. They're the real thing, Annie.'

And I have taken care of them. The box is in the studio. The paints it contains are seventh, eighth generation now. But I was never a watercolourist, not even as good as the great-aunts. I still try sometimes, for a kind of relaxation. It stimulates the brain and then comes an odd calming effect, recognising a result no better than expected. But the box is there and well used since the day I unwrapped it. I can still remember the astonishment, the sharp delight.

It was Julia, though, who gave me my first tube of oil paint. It was a single tube of vermilion and she had tied a brown label to its neck which said, 'For Annie. X.'

It was unlike her to bestow kisses, even on paper.

Thank you, Julia.

Chapter Twelve

Wim rings. He is coming to see me, he says. How can he promote my work if I don't do any? There is something wrong. He senses it. He has begun to worry about it. 'About you, Annie,' he says.

I'm fine, I tell him.

Afterwards I go to the studio and draw an angry face in charcoal. Looking at it later I begin to have a suspicion it is my own.

The piano child is finished. I ring up, leave a message with amiable Mrs Piano. She says kindly she's so pleased, she's longing to see it. It is clear that her opinion is generally of little account. After this I take the boat and row upriver, passing the swans, other people's gardens. One has a boat-house I covet. Further on the trees lean right over the water and under Cat Street bridge there is a lot of silt, good mud-pie stuff, that grounds me. Two hundred and fifty years ago Cat Street had two butchers, a fourth-rate alehouse and enough women to service all the bargees and keelmen and anyone else who dared risk a dose of clap. The bad end of town. Today it has the tranquillity of a postcard. The leaning cottages are almost genteel. Tourists take pictures of each other there before walking the few yards to the tea rooms for scones and cream. A definite improvement, says David. But so dull, says Annie.

On, nearly at the mill now. I can hear the soft slur of water in the sluice. Rowing becomes hard work. Well, awkward, bloody-minded little boat, isn't it, built by David in a shed when he was seventeen, trying out his father's woodworking tools. What he produced was the Jumblies' sieve. The sieve and I make wet progress into dappled shade where there is a whiff of cows, ivy, rotting oak. The mill is to be converted to luxury flats but for now glassless windows look down as I let the boat drift round in the current, borne away homeward. Nice to sit still, to glide along.

Funny, Julia never let me paint her. Didn't like photographs either.

I am passing the boat-house. I hardly dip the oars, the stream carries us along. Not bad, David. A good boat after all, in its own eccentric fashion.

Perhaps Julia feared, like ancient tribes, to put her soul in danger.

'Where've you been?' asks Sam when I go into the house. He has made a bacon sandwich and generously offers me a bit.

'You're always eating,' I accuse. 'Just to the mill.'

'You look exhausted.'

'That's Wim moaning on. And the picture.'

'The piano child?'

'Something else.'

'Good?'

'So far exasperation and a muddy purple background.'

The piano family stand in front of the picture. It is a good picture though nothing is ever perfect, there is always a brushstroke too many or too few. Claire twists a piece of hair round and round a finger. She looks a little startled as if she doesn't recognise herself. So what? Paintings are not photographs. I have been faithful to her but in the subtle way of an artist. Artist's heads are stuffed with all sorts and it comes out through their hands.

'Very nice,' says the father. He too is startled. On the other hand, it looks like his daughter, the piano is suitably prominent and he can see the whole thing's different, a talking point. He relaxes a little and smiles. Yes, all right. Very nice.

The mother looks at me. She understands what I saw. She says tentatively, 'She looks as if she might speak. As if she might suddenly get down from the piano stool, climb out of the picture.'

The father glares at her, thinking her stupid.

I offer them all coffee rather belatedly and am relieved when they refuse.

Gina is sent home from school with a nosebleed. She is delivered in a teacher's car at half-past one and I go to the door with a sandwich in one hand and chewing so that I give the impression of being slatternly and unconcerned. Gina makes apologetic noises into a wad of tissue. I take her in and fetch towels and tell her to keep still and take deep breaths and all will be well.

In twenty minutes all begins to be well. Her nose is revealed as bruised as well as bloody. I grow heated. Who did this? I demand. Miriam with a tennis racquet. It was an accident. Sam laughs rather heartlessly.

'You are a beast,' cries Gina indistinctly. 'Boys are useless.'

She feels betrayed and indignant. Noses are embarrassing. People stare. Brothers are unsympathetic. She is anxious about lying down in case the bleeding starts again. She rests sitting up on the sofa, propped among cushions, her legs up.

'Who did this?' David asks. He has come home to a litter of teacups and bowls of gory water.

'It was an accident.'

'Poor baby,' he says, stooping to kiss the top of Gina's rumpled head. Her bottom lip trembles.

'Don't cry,' I warn, tough-as-boots old mother. 'It'll bleed again.'

Sam comes in. 'Did you know you have half a dozen messages on the answerphone? One's from someone in Paris who wants you to paint his wife.'

'Wim will be pleased,' I say.

'You and Wim,' begins Greta. We have met at the Oyster for lunch and I can tell she wants to be provoking.

'There is nothing between me and Wim.'

'So you always say. Has David actually met him?'

'I think so. Once.'

To deflect her from the subject I tell her Gina is at home with two black eyes and a swollen nose.

'Poor Gina,' she says, but cavalierly, her mind elsewhere. She has children of her own and swollen noses are nothing.

We order sandwiches, insert ourselves in a corner. A popular pub, the Oyster. Greta always likes the noisy crush.

'Are you free this weekend?'

'I might be.'

'You've finished the picture.'

'I've started another. And David's had phone calls from the police in Munich. The corpse is dead but refusing to lie down, you might say.'

'I thought it had all been a mistake?'

'So did we all. But then some bright young constable pulled a thread that ran from Cologne to Munich and three times round Strasburg and then to an interesting

139

collection of offshore accounts and a business in the Philippines. Poor David's ageing by the minute.'

'A bit of excitement. Halingford's not exactly an ambitious solicitor's dream, is it?'

I decline to answer. The sandwiches arrive.

'This weekend,' says Greta. 'We can go away together.'

We range along the beach to clear our heads. I stride along leaving Greta scrambling. I feel out of sorts. It is the misery that descends when a picture is finished and another is going badly. It is like recovery after food poisoning, the skin tender, the mouth dry. I want to be alone. I want to remain silent.

'Annie ...' A protest. A clink of stones behind. In front the sea plunges and slides, a mass of steely blue. One of the local fishing boats is making a difficult passage home, throwing up spray.

Greta stands shivering. She never dresses for the weather.

'It's nearly summer inland,' she says. 'Why like the Arctic up here?'

'You chose the Oyster,' I remind her.

'I like the Oyster. I don't like this beach. Pebbles. And so much wind.'

'Then we should have gone straight home,' says callous big sister.

Because I am really thinking of the pictures, of the piano girl; I seem to hear my mother's voice. 'You've done the hands well. So few artists do hands well. And resting on the keys, braced, ready. Good. You always had perception.'

Then why can't I see Julia?

Greta drives me to our weekend hideaway, an old inn on the edge of salt marshes fifty miles away. There are plenty of salt marshes near home. Why more? Greta will only totter around in unsuitable heels and say her legs are cold. She does not wear country clothes and does not notice wildlife. Already she is worrying about what's happening at home without her. Pictures, music, mean very little to her. What do we ever find to talk about?

'Did you find anything to eat?' I ask David on Saturday evening.

'Gina and I scraped out the fridge. What about you?'

'Oh, you know. Greta would never stay anywhere without a world-class chef.'

'And what have you been doing?'

'Walking. I'm dressed for the Matterhorn and she waltzes along in deck shoes and a silk sweater.'

'Good?'

'So so.'

Is he missing me? Saturday is our evening for catching up, bills, worries, world events. Saturday is the two of us, log fires, Dowland.

'You took the box with you,' he says.

'I've nearly finished with it.'

'Thank God.'

Dowland, Sheppard, Purcell. They are in my head. I lie in a comfortable cold bed and make the notes soar into darkness. Sleep is elusive.

At Charleshall the light on the nursery landing burned all night. The glow was always there under the bedroom door. I would lie looking at it, listening to Julia's breathing as she slept. She slept with an old bear which she stuffed down out of sight so that Dukie, so that Judith, so that I wouldn't know. I don't remember if it had a name. It was never to be mentioned. So I never mentioned it. I was her friend and friends know what's what.

Shallow, even breaths. Don't go to sleep, Julia. There are so many questions. I need to ask about Judith, about the boy you married and divorced, about Philippe ... And why drive off the road? Did you drive off the road?

I sleep at last and dream of Julia. I am falling through space but I am holding Julia, her hair is in my face, tickling my nostrils. It is like riding the rocking horse together, something we seldom did, it was too uncomfortable, insecure, and she always made it rock so fast ... So fast. Stop, Ju. Stop. Stop.

And so she stops and leans forward to lay her head against the thin coarse mane.

'Oh, Annie, wouldn't it be wonderful to fly?'

Sunday morning, to amuse myself, I try ringing Wim. I trawl Europe with the numbers he has given me: his house in Delft, temporarily occupied by a cousin, his *tjalk* afloat in Amsterdam, somebody's apartment in Paris, a farmhouse near Grasse. No mobile, of course. He never gives his mobile number. 'This,' he always says, waving it about, 'is for me to call you.'

'Who is it please?' they all say, these strangers I disturb still half-asleep or eating breakfast or dressing to go out. Just say Annie rang. O.K., Annie rang, but who knows when he'll be here again ... He comes and goes. Annie who?

The cousin is furiously chatty. Workmen relaying the hall floor have found the entrance to a cellar. She is left with a gaping hole. She says Wim has always been charming but elusive, always absent during crises, always careless of possessions, money, women. He really only takes trouble over artists. Has he mentioned this potter, this girl in Antwerp? Certainly cousins can't compete, especially cousins on his

142

mother's side, practical pragmatic Flemish girls with big noses.

'So, are you one of his artists?' she demands at last.

'I'm afraid so.'

'Then find him for me and bloody ask him does he want the thing filled in.'

'What filled in?'

'The hole.' She has a pleasant, rasping voice and is dragging on a cigarette every other word.

'I'll ask,' I promise.

The afternoon is warm. Greta sits charmingly between lavender bushes while I sketch her in charcoal. She doesn't talk for once but sits upright, all attention. She has never posed for me before and is taking it too seriously. Or perhaps she is mocking me, mocking the necessity to keep still for so long, mocking the artist who must naturally take it too seriously. But she can't keep it up, she begins to walk about, bruising the lavender.

'Well?' she asks.

I look at my pad and see that I've drawn a discontented middle-aged woman, that the nose is wrong. I tear it up.

'Well nothing, apparently,' I say.

'You like Wim, don't you?' She doesn't seem upset about the picture, has already progressed a long way down some other path.

'What is all this about Wim? He's a charming man. There are too few, unluckily.' I'm not having her peering over the fence into my private life even if there's nothing to see.

'I haven't met one for years.'

I detect the vague restlessness that frequently drives women a little distracted. It is not that she wants to be away from small children, she simply wants to be out

143

among people. Among people she might meet someone whose thoughts linked with her own, whose language she understood. Thus could self-confidence, the heady joy of being desired, be nourished.

'Do you want me to try again?' I ask her, waving the charcoal.

'No. I'd rather go for a walk.'

'Then you walk, I'll stay here and draw.'

As soon as she has gone I put down the pad and lean back and bask in the sun.

I seem to see us always under the mulberry: Judith, Alain, Arlette flitting in and out with trays, dishes, glasses, warnings, exclamations. There is laughter. There is the tingling aromatic scent of Alain's cigarettes. Sometimes there are the boys, grubby, secretive, inhabiting a world that coincides with ours only at mealtimes. Rarely there is Julia. She is in the background or to one side, a slender mysterious figure in the dappled light, often with her head bowed, her face hidden. Now as then I feel the sharp momentary anguish of incomprehension. I don't understand her. I don't understand. She has never been so distant or so unkind.

'Are you awake?' demands Greta, and prods me to make sure.

'Why?'

'You'll be sunburned.'

'In April? In England?'

She reaches out and brushes a tentative hand across my hair. 'You always were so difficult,' she says.

David has bought himself new pyjamas which don't suit him, which would be perfectly decent and unremarkable on an old man ... But.

'You can't wear those,' I tell him. I am sitting on

144

the end of the bed trying to tame my hair.

He takes them off and attempts to prove he is not an old man yet, but mind his bad shin, he caught it on a filing cabinet, Bibs disappointingly unsympathetic, bruise like a crushed plum. And don't laugh. How does a woman expect a man to make love to her while she's laughing?

'I take it the weekend with Greta was bloody? You've not said a word about it,' he says.

I am making a salad and listening to Scarlatti which he thinks is tinkly and too clever.

'Bloody.'

'I don't know why you go.'

He sits at the table, chopping tomatoes. A big heavy man, recently much perplexed by human failings, his and everyone else's. He was made to feel a fool by slick young policemen in leather jackets. His hair is turning grey quietly, the way I wish mine would. He looks ordinary and kindly and if he had an affair would keep it quiet and afterwards not expect me to be reasonable.

'It's like Julia,' I say stupidly.

'What's like Julia?'

'My having to stand by wondering what the hell's going on.'

'Haven't you finished with that box yet?'

'Almost.'

'You say that every time I ask you.'

'Then don't ask.'

Chapter Thirteen

I like to use plenty of paint but what with scraping and scratching I sometimes get back to bare canvas. This is usually the consequence of a vile mood. Today I have painted my way out of one tantrum and into another. And for what?

Here is Julia on the rocking horse, leaning forward. The hand is not right. Yes, hands are difficult. I've a good mind to tip the thing in the river. The mouth is not right either. There is no point in going on. Struggling like a beginner at a first life class is only permissible in the preliminary sketches, not for now, now when I should be laying on paint with confidence, intelligence. I don't feel intelligent. And I find I can't paint from memory. Memory flickers and shifts like light under the mulberry. Julia is just a tall slender girl running beneath trees, seen from behind. All I know for sure is the heavy bobbed hair, glossy dark.

It is raining today, a monotonous rain. It soothes and provokes at the same time. I clean my brushes – yes, I spend a great deal of my life cleaning brushes, they are my tools, expensive – and then fling on an old raincoat, go out. I walk up the hill into the town and then cut through the churchyard and go down the steps to the river and the water meadows. When I return, having achieved nothing but a stitch and wet feet, I find Wim on the doorstep.

He wants coffee, food, and to talk about an exhibition in Antwerp. He is enthusiastic about the former, doubtful about Antwerp. He considers it an inferior sort of place, it once gave him and his *tjalk* a bad time, something to do with a lock, an engine failure. Besides, it reminds him of his cousins, those tough big-nosed girls with splendid tempers and thick gym-mistressy legs. Wim likes to think of himself as quite-frankly-Dutch, slow, polite, competent. If not, then European, whatever that is. He doesn't bother with the house in Delft, which he inherited; he lives mostly on his old barge and can drone on for hours about lee-boards and gaffs, and the minute the latest girlfriend finds him out she packs her bags. There is no competing with a boat. And life on the water is an acquired taste anyway. And an old *tjalk* is not a gin palace and Amsterdam is not Cannes.

'I hear you talked to Kitty,' he says.

'About the hole, yes.'

'Medieval undercroft.'

'Large hole, according to Kitty. And at the foot of the stairs. Most inconvenient.'

'They'll put in a trap door.'

He and Kitty practically grew up together. The first bike he ever rode was hers. She taught him to navigate by the stars. He thought of her as his sister but she had four sisters of her own so sometimes he felt over-whelmed by managing women. They were all opinionated, forthright and clever, just rather too many. He once pushed two of them into some canal, an incident which subsequently involved the Dutch rescue services, much shouting and a copybook display of artificial respiration.

'So what have you been doing?' he asks. He has a

147

plane to catch in three hours. Is there time for a proper lunch?

He is allowed in the studio because pictures are his business. He turns over canvases, then sketches, lightly, briskly. Nothing is disturbed, nothing hauled out of place. He is neat and careful. He understands these arrangements are personal, sacred. Some artists he knows scream if he turns round anything with its face to the wall.

He likes the piano child.

'These people are getting a good picture. Do they know?'

'I think they'd rather have something conventional in pastels.'

'This too meaty, huh? She looks abused.' He is considering, head on one side.

'She's made to practise till her fingers drop off. How would you look?'

He carries on, picking here and there. I have nothing seriously good enough for a major exhibition. I've been working myself silly to finish the commissions and only the piano child and a couple of others have been in any way exceptional.

But then he walks round the easel and pauses.

'Ah,' he sighs.

He slouches there a while, sucking his lips. He is hugely tall and thin and he wears expensive casual clothes that crease elegantly. I notice there is a reddish streak in his beard.

'How's Sonya?' I ask. It won't be Sonya now, of course, but Ilse or Yvonne or Isabel.

'Do you know, the woman likes boats.' Do I detect anxiety? 'She made me buy a new cooker and half a ton of stainless steel shackles. She says I need better anchors. She is an inexhaustible fund of advice.'

'She's still around then?'

'Too much, Annie dear. She strides straight off the catwalk into an apron and rubber gloves, model to *hausfrau* before you can blink twice. Not only that, she insists we sail. Now she says my standing rigging won't hold up a matchstick, what I am going to do about it? She'll cost me a fortune before she's done.'

'Then it's the boat she loves, not you.'

'No doubt.'

We eat French stick with everything we can find in the fridge stuffed inside. He drinks pints of coffee. He says he wants to see the portrait of Julia when it's finished. He says he might buy.

'It's not even half finished. It may never be finished. It's not for sale.'

'I want it on my wall.'

'The wall of a *tjalk*?'

'Why should you object?'

We eat on. The rain falls with more purpose and a sudden darkness invades the house. I turn on the lights and his blond head dazzles. He is still chasing salami round his teeth. He says, 'She intrigues me. Who is she? Another child prodigy?'

'It's from memory. She's dead. Someone from long ago.'

'I like women with black hair.' He glances apologetically at my rusted curls. 'You know. Nineteen-twenties. Straight bob.' His hands sketch around his own face. 'Good bones. Boyish.'

'She wasn't your sort. Hated parties.'

He sits still, considering. He is a kindly man and doesn't blunder about people's tender spots. He is wondering if the picture is part of a grief process. Well, fine. Let old Annie get it out of her system, he can wait. He reaches for the coffee pot.

'You cared for her?' is all he asks.

'I don't know.'

149

'You were angry when you painted.'

'Nothing went right.'

He leaves the subject alone. Tricky subject. He begins to talk of other things, exhibitions, balance sheets. He wants the piano child and two others for Antwerp, and, if possible, Julia. He writes all this down on the back of an envelope in his clear looping script, underlines every other word, puts it in front of me and tells me he will ring at the end of the week. Then he tells me I'm looking peaky. He has picked up this word somewhere and wants to use it, wants to enjoy it. English vernacular. He has almost no accent so it sounds all right but I tell him it's the wrong word, I've looked in the glass and made my own assessment; try haggard.

'Not sleeping?' He sounds genuinely concerned.

'Things on my mind.'

'Then paint.' He stoops to kiss the top of my head. 'Paint, Annie. Paint.'

Before he goes he has another look at Julia. She has moved him and he wants to understand why.

'So subdued. The palette. Dim. Why such gloomy purple, Annie? You won't forget I want it, will you? Is this a real horse?'

'No, of course not.'

'But she's too old for toys.'

'It was big. It was more than a toy. And old. It had rockers, not one of those safety stands. If you went fast it was frightening, it moved across the floor.'

He puts an arm round my shoulders. 'She cause you much grief, this Julia?' And then, remembering. 'Hell, my flight.'

But he knows I haven't answered. He kisses me goodbye warmly but abstractedly.

'Well?'

'Yes,' I say.

*

The summerhouse has a little wooden ball at the apex of its thatched roof which once, in a kind of fit, Sam and I gilded. Today, because the sun is shining, I get up a ladder and repaint it. Crouched against the reed, brush in hand, I look away across the marsh to the distant woods where, when we first came here, you could hear nightingales. In between, green water meadows, the straggling lines of the dikes, cattle moving slowly from one favoured place to another. Below, there are the swans and the reflection of the gold ball in the water.

I should be painting. Instead I am gilding an old tumbledown summerhouse, scratching my knees, getting spiders in my hair. I cannot face the studio, the easel. I cannot face Julia. It seems impossible to retrieve her from the past – and for God's sake, why should I want to? She is shadowy, almost lost. Then let her go. Better that way. Certain things are better left alone, better left ... I steady the little pot of gold paint.

Some things.

I close my eyes.

When I open them there is a kestrel hovering over the reed beds. The town clock chimes. Bibs will be carrying in David's coffee. All's right with the world. We lead uneventful, circumscribed lives, are content, complacent even.

Julia ... a ... a ...

All that afternoon there was a racket in the woods. Juliaaaa ... a ... a ... Judith, Arlette, even the old goat woman, the mad aunt. Up and down, up and down. Julia, Juliaaaa. I was left at the house with instructions: if this happens, do this, if not, do the other, keep an eye on the boys, if Alain comes tell him Julia is missing ... so on, so on. 'I know you're sensible,' said Judith. She was white, her eyes dark and staring already with shock although as yet no shocks had come. They were for later perhaps. 'Someone must be here in case ...' she said. In case Julia came back, walking in calmly, asking 'Why all the fuss? I only went for a walk.'

The windows were shuttered as usual during the heat of the day. The kitchen tap dripped. From far away came the thin shrieking of the boys at some bloodthirsty game. There was a lizard on the table under the mulberry. I sat on the wall, kicking my heels. It was so hot. Why would anyone want to walk about when it was so hot? Even under the trees there would be no relief. A storm was coming. The sky was an intense and glassy blue.

She had gone out not long before lunch. Arlette had raised the alarm, Arlette who had exaggerated Monsieur Blanchard's peccadilloes but now wondered if ... If. Julia still out, Heaven knew where, lunch on the table, no sign of her. Madame? 'She'll come back,' said Judith quietly. She had been tried before, left guessing, scoured by anxiety until she looked bloodless, worn out in the struggle to remain calm.

Two hours passed and still no Julia.

'She's sitting up a tree,' I told Arlette in the kitchen. 'She wants everyone to be worrying about her.' It seemed to me Julia had spoiled this holiday enough, there could be no question of sympathy.

'Anything might have happened,' said Arlette darkly. She too drew secret and questionable enjoyment from such ridiculous dramas.

'No,' I insisted. I suddenly thought her ridiculous. It was extraordinary how some adults could be so ridiculous. 'No, she's just up a tree.'

Silence. The dripping tap. The boys had gone

deeper into the valley, I couldn't hear them any more. The lizard had flicked off the table and darted into a crevice in the wall. The heat was heavy. It seemed to press down on my head. I had difficulty breathing. Once I thought I heard, far in the distance, a thin cry of Juliaaaa.

There were no messages to send because nothing happened. Nobody called. Alain didn't come. Well, he was in the village with a full surgery, all unsuspecting. I fetched my sketch book and tried to draw but nothing came, it was as if my hand was paralysed. I suddenly saw Julia dead, crumpled on the thick soft ground beneath the trees.

'Where is everyone?' she asked. She was in the doorway, but I had to blink, the burning light was so strong. For a moment I couldn't see her properly at all and then she moved and I noticed her torn skirt, the scratches on her thin hands. Her face was tired and bruised and secretive, but then it often was.

'Where've you been? Everybody's frantic.' And I watched her for the faint signs of quiet pleasure. This is what she has wanted, to cause a fuss. This is why she stays out too long or goes to the village without letting anyone know, knowing Judith would be crippled by anger and concern; or perhaps not knowing but wanting to find out.

'I've just been walking.' There was no trace of triumph.

'But where? Didn't you hear them calling?'

'I didn't hear anything.'

'I've got to ring the bell by the shrine to let them know you're back,' I told her. 'Arlette said they'd hear that wherever they were.'

I saw she had withdrawn to some other place. No Dukie here, no kittens to play with in the stableyard, so she has gone inside herself.

'Go on then,' she said, far, far away, indifferent, removed.

I started forward, thought of something, stopped next to her. She smelled leafy, foresty. 'You won't disappear again?'

She came back momentarily from wherever she had gone. Astonishingly, she leaned forward, kissed my forehead where the tendrils of hair stick hotly. Then she gave my messy pigtail a tug.

'Old carroty Annie,' she said.

Here is Julia, and here am I, brush in hand. And I cannot see her, cannot bring her to life. She is as dead on the canvas as she is in her grave in France. Even now, recalling that unexpected, impersonal embrace, the way she broke away abruptly and ran upstairs, I hold the brush close to my chest, know I will get nothing done today. Or any day?

She was pale, but then she was always pale. She had a bruise on one cheekbone, bits of leaf in her hair. In my head I can see her vaguely, a shape moving. I know about the bruise, the hair, yet her face is not properly clear. I could not explain or paint the relationship between mouth or nose. Then I was mystified by where she had been, what she had been doing, and now I'm simply mystified. The incident happened. I was there. She smelt of the woods, of heat. She kissed me. But I can't see her. I can't see her on the canvas.

Why try? This is a *Route sans Issue*, Annie. *That* was the sign, propped against a boulder, on the track to the farm. I used to run past it with the milk can and clouds of little blue butterflies would rise from the grasses. 'Blanchard. *Route sans Issue*.'

'What a baby you are,' Julia said. 'Running all the way. You think there are bogeymen in the woods.'

'I don't.'

'They why run. I've seen you.'

'Why don't you come with me?'

'If I can't go by myself I don't want to go at all. Why should I? Nobody trusts me even to fetch the milk. They think I go there to let ...'

'No, they think it's Monsieur.'

'They think I let him.'

'Let him what?'

'Whatever.' She turned away.

And I suddenly knew. I knew she was as innocent as I was, that Monsieur Blanchard did nothing, that all Arlette's fears were groundless. But she never told Judith this, or anyone, never explained. 'I got lost,' was all they could get out of her, even Alain, who held on bravely in the teeth of her sullenness. Then what was the bruise? Nothing. She had fallen. There were plenty of places to fall, so who could disprove it? After a while she began to seem like a wraith. Her skin had paled and paled, the bruises had spread, her hair had grown more tangled. She said nothing, unless 'Yes' and 'No' and 'I got lost' counted as something. 'I'm perfectly all right. Why don't they leave me alone?' Was the only proper sentence she uttered, and she said it to me where I hovered in the doorway, not knowing if I was welcome to go in.

'Annie,' and Judith held out an arm. She drew me to her. I was a relief, outside the drama, quite astonishingly ordinary and innocent. It was with relief she hugged me.

'I want to go upstairs,' said Julia.

'To bed, darling? I'll come.'

'I don't want you to come.'

Julia moved stiffly. She could have been an old woman.

'You'd better go with her, Annie,' Alain said. 'She might tell you ... She might tell you what happened.'

155

'Nothing happened. She fell out of a tree,' I said.

'I don't believe her,' Judith had struck her hands together as if she was in pain. 'How could she get lost? And if she did, why not tell us about it? Any other child would say well, I went down here and turned there and then there was a farm and then woods ... And then I didn't know where I was. But not Julia. Julia says nothing.'

'She doesn't lie,' I pointed out.

'Not saying anything is sometimes as good as lying,' cried Judith.

Alain crossed the room and put his arm round her. 'She's fine,' he murmured. 'She likes to give you frights.'

'But I don't *know* ... I never *know* ...'

I climbed the stairs and found Julia face down on her bed but not asleep. Her eyes were closed but she was tense, prepared.

'I suppose they think I'll tell you everything.'

'But there isn't anything to tell.'

'I know. I just got lost.'

There was a warm twilight in the room, the smell of wood, old board floors, old beams. I sat and plucked at the fringe of her bedspread.

'Were you frightened?'

'No. But it seemed miles.'

'Where did you go?'

'I don't know. Another valley. It was just trees, trees and trees. I heard a dog barking.' Her eyes were open now. It seemed an effort for her to remember.

'Did you climb a tree?'

'I might have done.' She would never confess to falling. There was honour at stake. I had always been the better climber.

'Your mother was really frightened,' I told her.

'Was she?'

156

She closed her eyes again.

'I hear Mademoiselle Julia got lost in the woods,' said Monsieur Blanchard when I went for the milk the next day.

'Yes.'

Our eyes met. I suddenly knew that he knew what was said about him. My face grew red, redder.

'Funny girl.' He tapped a finger twice against his forehead. 'But then,' and he shrugged, smiling. 'Funny age, fourteen, eh? For some.'

I ring Monique. I am sorry it has been such a long time. No, there's nothing in the box except old letters, school reports, photographs of happier times, some rings, a bracelet. Would she like the rings? No. She has the diamond engagement ring Philippe bought. There are no others she knows or cares about. But it is kind of me, she says stiffly, to think of such a thing.

There is nothing in the box then, I tell her, of interest to her family. There is nothing of Philippe, of his, of him, of the marriage.

'Good,' she says, thinking aloud. To cover this lapse she becomes brisk, even censorious. All that fuss about a small box and just because no one knew what might be in it, but then Julia ...

'Yes?' I ask. 'Julia?'

'Could be a little strange. You said yourself. Difficult. Difficult to know, difficult to help.'

'Did she need help?'

'I thought she was lonely sometimes, stuck up there in that house. She didn't go out much, seemed to have few interests. She lived for Philippe.'

I feel the strain of this conversation is too great, though it is really quite ordinary and there are no double meanings intended. I want to put down the receiver, put away Monique, the grief I know she feels, about which I can do nothing.

'You see,' she is continuing, 'we were afraid she might have given you something not hers to give. Can you understand? One could never say, ah, Julia would never do such a thing, such or such a thing ... One was never sure. Only that I believe she would never have left Philippe. She was ...'

'In love.'

'Possessive.'

'No, she would never have taken anything that wasn't hers,' I tell her. But of course to Monique Julia was certainly a thief, she had robbed her of her only child, taking him over that precipice and into the dark.

'And is the house sold yet?'

'No, not yet. The lawyer deals with all that. We don't take a close interest.'

I realise that now shock is wearing off they find it better not to think of Julia. Only when it's necessary will they mention her name. Jooliaa. And perhaps they will lie a little, for decency's sake: she and Philippe, so happy ... They will not remember what she looked like or how she spoke or whether they had ever felt any fondness for her. She will simply be a name. Best like that probably, best for everyone. Otherwise only bitterness, the constant thought if only ... If only this, if only the other. If only Philippe had never met her.

'I must go.' I despise my bright, false voice, but there is nothing I can do about it. 'You're sure about the rings?'

'I know nothing about any rings. They must have belonged to her family, to her mother. And not very valuable, you say? Just odds and ends, trinkets. She never cared much for jewellery, never wore any for everyday.' I hear the faintest condescension, the faintest trace of pity. How like Julia to leave a friend

158

such things. 'Sentimental value, I expect,' she adds encouragingly when I remain silent.

But that is something neither of us will ever know.

Chapter Fourteen

Strange people, painters. I usually say I'm a painter, saves a lot of trouble. They think you're an interior decorator, a harmless occupation. Say artist and there comes the instant reek of disorder and rebellion and sloppy morals. Besides, who makes real money out of art? A favoured few. So – disorderly, rebellious, promiscuous and poor. Such things should hardly be tolerated.

'Goodbye then,' says David, off to work. I have already been in the studio an hour and he has put his head round the door. He can see how it is.

'Goodbye to you.'

Sensibly, he retreats.

Later, when Wim rings and says for God's sake Annie finish the girl with the purple mud background, this being fresh in his mind and still troubling him, I become shrill. I don't know if I can, I tell him. I don't know. Just leave it. Don't mention it. He ignores all this, carries on cheerfully about whether or not to frame the piano child. Yes? No? Not sure? The gallery in Antwerp is splendid, but hanging there is always a buggeration, involving ladders, difficulties with lighting. He sounds breathless with enthusiasm but I suspect he is just chasing his breakfast croissant round his teeth. There are tinny noises behind him and low buzzing. When asked where he is he says on the quay by the *tjalk* and it's raining. And can I do a portrait of Sonya one day? Better make it before my prices go up again. She has a bony head, he says, the sort I like, great pits of eyes, solid no-nonsense chin. She talks and talks, emotions, politics, wombs. He is afraid she's going to be permanent. Annie? Still listening? He fades out under a noise like iron girders being dropped.

Painting young women is difficult. Later, when experience has scraped away at the pretty blandness, character shows through, serene or aggressive. I am a little afraid of Sonya. She is a model and knows how to wear masks; she is young and will probably want to look her best. Back in the studio I look at Julia and think, this is impossible, more impossible than any of Wim's girls. She felt herself unloved. How do I paint that? But I must. Such things are not revealed by photographs, but ought to be by painters, by me, by friend Annie, by this other child who shared the rocking horse, kept quiet about the teddy bear, welcomed her back from that walk in the woods.

I take her off the easel and work on something else. I work furiously, in hope. Often this sort of thing comes out well. Today I get in a muddle with too much white and then too much linseed and the glass jug doesn't look like a glass jug and all the colours are strike-your-eye. Too much, not enough, and all a waste of precious paint. But then ... Presumably writers waste whole forests, scribbling, despairing, screwing up.

'Take you out for a sandwich?' asks Sam, who has sidled up to scratch on the door.

'I'm not dressing up,' I tell him.

'When do you ever?'

So we go to a smoky pub in the town and eat beef

161

sandwiches with good hot mustard and he tells me how he would die if he had to design shopping centres for a living. I wonder if he's working up to tell me next that he wants to drop architecture, but then he swoops away with inspired ideas for the housing of the future, all timber, glass and eco-friendly plumbing.

'So come on, what about your box?' he demands eventually, unexpectedly, having fetched himself another beer.

'Nearly finished.'

'You're always saying that. And you're always ratty these days. And not painting well. Dad's worried.' He drinks some beer, thinks a little harder. 'Why did she leave you a box of old papers?'

'I think she wanted me to understand.'

'Understand what?'

'Her.'

Crazy old women, he is thinking. He wipes foam from his top lip. 'Any clue as to why she never got in touch?'

'They might not have given my letters to her straight away. It crossed my mind. There's a letter from the Major to her later that summer, the summer Judith died, and it's addressed to a private nursing home. I wonder if she had a breakdown of some kind. These days an army of do-gooders would take her in hand, therapy, counselling, mustn't bottle it up, Julia, that sort of thing. Then it was stiff-upper-lip, pretend it never happened. By the time she came home home wasn't Charleshall any more, the Major had taken off to some estate in Dorset, all sheep and no shooting, much smaller house, all mod cons. There's a picture of it with the wedding photos, her first marriage. They had a marquee on the lawn.'

'But why no note?' Sam protests. 'Why never write at all? She could have written afterwards. It wouldn't have mattered how long afterwards, would it? Anything. Just a line. You were supposed to be friends.'

'Well,' I say, pushing my glass towards him. 'Julia was always different.'

'But apart from the breakdown, if that's what it was,' he says when he comes back from the bar, 'what was she doing those next few years?'

'She was sent to a school in Dorset. They asked her to leave. Rudeness, general attitude to work, definitely not a model pupil. By that time the Major had remarried. And who knows what that Mrs Hawsley was like? Julia was packed off to be finished. But there was more trouble. The Major fetched her back himself. She wrote a letter of apology to the stepmother about it but it was never sent ... There's the wedding invitations next, everybody smiling. I don't know. I just don't know, Sam. But I think she was unhappy.'

'Unhinged,' he says calmly. 'I still don't see why she couldn't have written you a note.'

But we never wrote notes. We wedged twigs and leaves in the bark of trees, built tiny cairns of stones, tied slippery horse hairs on branches. There was a code: all clear, meet usual place, look up oak tree, go to stables, kitchen, rocking horse. Each feather, each pebble had a meaning. The box has a meaning. The truth about Julia is in the box, as elusive as a handful of water. In a moment all that is left is the shine of wetted skin.

Of course, I have not told Sam everything. I have not told David everything.

I have never told anyone.

The piano child is dry. David says they'll like it in Antwerp but does the father know? He might not approve. He might forbid it.

163

'He hasn't paid me yet,' I say, not in the mood for trifling.

'Well, mind Wim doesn't sell it to someone else.'

He has only been gone half an hour when Bibs drops in for some papers he has forgotten.

'It's all this police business,' she says. 'It's unsettled him.'

'He's reassessing the business, Halingford. He didn't like being treated like a dumb small-town lawyer and he's wondering if it's too late to be a smart big city one.'

'Silly fool,' says Bibs comfortingly.

I take her to see the piano child which she looks at for a long time without saying anything. Then, 'Poor kid. Lucy had a friend in primary school looked like that, a girl whose ma was convinced she could win gold medals ice skating. Every spare moment they were off to some rink a hundred miles away. She had a Russian trainer, I remember. Never had time to play with the other children. It all came to a sudden end anyway, don't know why. I know she kept bursting into tears at school. They took her away and that was the last we heard. I bet she's anorexic now. And who's this?' She has seen Julia, stares at her, perplexed.

'Someone I knew a long time ago. It won't come right.'

Bibs, who has an answer for everything, looks from me to Julia and back again.

'Perhaps you don't want it to,' she says.

I mix colours and select brushes and sit and stare out at the garden and under my breath I swear and mutter and recite verse and names of artists in alphabetical order from the fourteen hundreds.

Now and then I walk up to the easel.

164

And this is Annie Somerville at her worst, cantan-
kerous, crabbed, incompetent. Nothing going right.
Catch a glimpse of her through the windows and what
do you see? Hair like a bush, streaked with that damn
grey, with ultramarine too probably, cross little eyes,
the general look of a Norn dressed up in a painting
apron.

And that, that on the canvas, isn't Julia.

Route sans Issue.

I'm not going to struggle any more. I am giving up.

I wear black velvet and red silk for Antwerp. 'I
despair of you,' says Gina. She makes me dress up so
that she can tweak and tug about and criticise, and she
puts my hair in a sort of bun and doubles up giggling
and undoes it and says she's glad she's not coming,
she wouldn't want anyone to think we belonged
together.

'Well thanks,' I say.

Antwerp is dull and warm. 'Nearly summer,' they
say hopefully in the hotel. By the time I am due at the
gallery it is raining and I have to borrow an umbrella
from reception. Reception is appalled I'm not taking a
taxi. But I am used to walking and I love being out on
the streets of an unknown town.

'Your legs are wet,' reproaches Wim.

'I stepped in a puddle.'

He ushers me in. All is as I expected, sophisticated,
beautifully hung, a triumph. A great many people have
come. I hardly know anybody, perhaps one or two. I
shake hands with an artist whose signature I would
recognise. Someone wants to buy the piano child. In
the end, although it is quite obviously not for sale, we
have five offers. They are all more than I shall receive
from Claire's father.

'You see?' says Wim.

'I charged the usual price.'

'Time it rose a little then.'

I do sell the picture of the two children. They are Greta's youngest. The technique is rather crude, I think, but I was painting so fast, and there is something, I've caught something. Oliver is just about to scrunch off his sunhat and throw it in the rock pool. Claudia is patiently prodding sea anemones with a stick. There is blinding sunlight, hot sand, the impression of frustration just about to break through all this tremendous concentration. Not bad, Annie.

'And I've just sold the old man,' Wim tells me, bringing me a sandwich because he worries I never eat anything. The old man is Harry Moy in his punt, disgruntled. The wind was cold, his wife had told him off, he didn't want to pose. 'Bloody nuisance all you women,' he said. In the picture he looks like someone with a lot of fight left in him.

In the evening we repair to Wim's *tjalk* which he sailed round with difficulty owing to all this defective rigging. People talk art and culture in general and anything else of interest, crammed in until one expects the boat to sink. The air is thick with smoke. Kitty is here. She tells me more of the saga of the floor, the hole, the trap door. She is mildly abusive about Wim's competence as a sailor. 'Good thing he has Sonya,' she asserts. And here is Sonya, just back from a modelling trip to Cuba, sleeping between bouts of being the perfect hostess. She is tall and bold and indeed has beautiful bones. Several men make rather pathetic passes, but she brushes them away gently as if they were importuning children. She has long broad capable hands, I notice. Good for hauling on ropes?

In lulls, when I have elbow room, I sketch her. She has a habit, when amused, of throwing back her head, flaring her nostrils. I don't think she knows she does this. It is eccentric but endearing. She rarely laughs aloud. It is clear that, like most people here, she speaks several languages more than competently.

'Well?' asks Wim.

'I don't know what she sees in you,' I tell him.

Later, just before he takes me back to the hotel, I take a fresh sheet of paper and let my hand wander, draw whatever comes. What comes is another face, younger, prettier, more vulnerable. The black fringe has been pushed aside and the eyes for once are fearless, questioning.

Hello, Julia.

I am in a hotel room in Antwerp. It is just an ordinary room, modern, anonymous. It does not look out on to water. It is not up a picturesque side street. Its tidiness, even the furniture arranged with precision, has shamed me into folding my clothes over the back of a chair, into hanging the silk and velvet in the wardrobe. I have put my shoes neatly by the bed.

It is three in the morning. There hardly seems any point in sleeping even if I could. It is past time for evasion too. I am tired and sober and a little chilly and I sit on the bed and hold the sketch of Julia. In a way, I suppose, she sits beside me. At long last. And she says, 'Do you remember, Annie?'

And I do.

It was the day Alain had lent me the book on Monet. Judith had badgered him sweetly about it for some days. 'The child's mad about art,' she had said. She made him promise to bring it. And he was a man who kept his promises, so he did. Before breakfast, on the way to a patient on a remote farm, he had left it on the kitchen table.

'For you, M'selle Annie,' said Arlette.

I picked it up, held it tightly to my flat chest, dipped my head to smell its pages. They smelt of his cigarettes, brought him before me, his lined face, his grave, courteous manner.

'They all make a fuss of you,' said Julia when I showed it to her. She was still in bed, turned her face into the pillow.

'No, they don't.'

'They talk to you. Mother does. He does. He takes you for walks. Now he's bringing you books.'

'I have to give it back.'

'I expect he'll let you have it.'

'But it's a huge book. Expensive.'

She suddenly turned, hauled herself up in the bed. 'They so love little Miss Goody-Goody, don't they? You're always so well behaved, reading your books, drawing your pictures.' She bent her head forward. Her hair swung down to hide her face. For weeks now she has been hiding her face.

'Why do you always have to be so horrible?' I asked. It was the first time for ages I had challenged her.

'I'm not horrible. You are.'

'Sometimes ... sometimes I hate you,' I said.

But later she seemed to make an effort, spoke to Arlette, asked after my mother when the post brought a letter. 'Your mother's clever,' she said. 'And interesting. And fun.'

'But you never come to stay. You hardly know her.'

'Perhaps I will. Come to stay. Would you have me?'

'You know we would.'

Time passed. I sat with the book under the mulberry. Since the day she got lost Julia had stayed in the house. She slept or sunbathed or wandered aimlessly about. This morning Arlette had taken the boys to the village to buy them ice-cream, Judith has

168

gone walking by the river. A moment ago her straw hat had just been visible. In half an hour she would be back to make the salad for lunch and I would be able to sit on the kitchen table and ask questions. I want to be a painter, I would tell her. But how? I was so excited and so ignorant. I knew nothing. I only knew I must ... I must. But where did one start? Where did one go?

Time passed. It seemed to me she should have returned by now. I wandered down the slope towards the trees and the river. The air was warm and fragrant under the oaks. My head was full of Monet, of light on water, light on faces, light through leaves. I wanted to paint like that, to understand like that. I wanted brush and paint and canvas ...

I could hear the water, bubbling and rushing. I could hear Judith's voice, unusually harsh, 'Don't be so silly, Julia.' I came to the last of the trees, hesitated.

They were standing by the rocky narrows, the deepest water. They were very near the edge.

'You love Annie more than me,' cried Julia, shrill, ridiculously shrill.

Don't go any nearer, don't breathe, better go back, Annie.

And Julia pushed her mother into the river.

Chapter Fifteen

I have brought the box out to the summerhouse and I have emptied it on to the wobbly rustic bench. The summerhouse smells of tarred wood and honeysuckle and river. I sit awhile, looking down at the mess. Then I begin to sift and sort, carefully, imposing order, sequence: childhood, girlhood, maturity. There is no way to stop time, it piles up and piles up. Here is Julia as a baby and then with me in the school photo; soon she is the bland smooth face at the Swiss finishing school. Here she is the devastated young daughter of the drowned woman, now a nakedly hostile Julia in a passport photograph, hair scraped back, lips set. Here is the wedding group again. Who could ever know what they were all thinking? Except Julia. I know what Julia was thinking: I want to go home to Dukie, to the rocking horse. But there is no Charleshall now, no Dukie, no refuge.

Had she loved this boy? Perhaps she had. And perhaps she wanted children and lost them. God knows the effect such things have. I can tell nothing from these scraps, these scribblings by strangers, these school reports and sad letters and faded photographs. What do they all mean? Did Julia really give it to me, this box of memories, for a purpose? Or because she was moody and tired and suddenly sentimental? I shall never know. She just packed up her life and put it by labelled 'For Annie'. Her friend Annie. Never ever not friends. That was what she used to say sitting up in the oak tree at Charleshall, nine years old, probably just over some silly tussle: 'We'll never ever not be friends, will we, Annie? Never ever.' No passion in her voice, no affection. She simply made the statement, as far as she was concerned, the truth. And 'Look, I've got some chocolate from Dukie,' fishing in a pocket, sharing it out. In the shade her hair was matt black, extinguished, her face mysterious.

It's no good, Ju. I don't understand.

Look, this is me sitting on the wall under the mulberry. I look pathetically young. I am wearing one of Judith's hats, a white cotton thing with the brim pushed up at the front. It reveals a hot, exhausted face. I must have run up from the *bassin*. There are damp curls of hair against my cheek. And here is Judith by the river, the boys in pirate eye patches, Arlette feeding the hens. Everything from a distance, very slightly out of focus. There are no pictures of Alain, the Blanchards, the old goat woman, of Julia herself. There is only the newspaper report: 'Englishwoman drowns in accident.' 'The husband is stricken with grief,' it says, 'called from important work in England to the scene of disaster. The children are being consoled by villagers.' Then there is the letter from the stepmother saying she is sorry the Major left nothing for Julia in his will, he had felt the boys needed money more. It is a prim, careful letter, and false. And there are my two letters, Julia where are you, the cry into silence.

It is a beautiful day. Leaning back, face to the sun, I don't look any more at Julia's life on the seat beside me. The river slips by, bubbling a little over some

171

obstruction under the willow. On the far bank are the cattle, placid, switching away flies. My neighbour has started his mower. Over on the house the climbing rose has a white bud, the first. It is always early, that rose, will be cut down by late May frosts.

'You love Annie more than me.'

I can hear her voice, strong and despairing but high, so high ... 'You love Annie Annie Annie ...'

A scream, a splash. I can't hear the scream now. It has been absorbed by time. Or perhaps splash and scream were simultaneous and I heard neither properly, having put my hands over my ears. Or perhaps, hitting her head on the rock, Judith hardly had time to cry out. I remember I began to run, kept running. I remember feeling sick and that the hill seemed steep and the house far away. My lungs hurt and hurt. Once I had to stop, bent double with nausea and stitch.

And under the mulberry Arlette was shaking out a clean white cloth for the table and the boys were leaning out of their upstairs window asking if there would be strawberries. I flung myself down by the wall where I had left Monet, my breath jerking in and out, my plait coming undone. To avoid looking at Artlette I picked it out, combed my hair through my fingers.

'You're quite pretty,' said Arlette.

'Not really. It's the colour of carrots.' I held out a strand of hair, still not looking at her. '*Comme les carottes*,' I said.

She laughed, went in for cutlery. The cloth was dazzlingly white. Small insects settled on it, a mulberry leaf. I did not think of what I had seen. I didn't believe what I had seen. There was a step and I felt breathless again, knowing it was Alain.

He came from the house, smiling. His eyes were

lost in wrinkles. He sat on one of the iron chairs. 'And how is Monet?'

Arlette and Alain were the ones who searched for Judith. Lunch was delayed. In fact we were never to eat it. As I stood under the mulberry looking down I could hear them calling, 'Madame!', 'Judith!', and I could see Julia sitting on the edge of the *bassin*, leaning forward a little as if she were studying her reflection in the water.

There was no phone in the house. Arlette, white and silent, bundled us – Julia, the boys, myself – into Judith's car and drove erratically to the village where she thrust us into Alain's kitchen.

'Something has happened. Look after them,' were her peremptory words to the housekeeper, an angular old woman in black.

'But what's happened? Where's Mummy?' cried Georgie.

'Be quiet,' commanded Arlette. 'Be good.' She went to use the telephone in the surgery.

Everything would be all right, said the old woman. She repeated this several times without conviction.

'But why do we have to stay here?' Tim was clutching Georgie. In crises they always clung together.

'I'll be back soon,' announced Arlette, whirling in, touching the boys on their cheeks, going out. We heard the car drive away.

An hour passed. We could not eat, nor speak, nor did we look at each other. But some time later the old woman brought us hot chocolate and little almond biscuits. I can see them now, tiny golden drops, and I can taste the sweetness of the sugar, the bitterness of the almonds as they dissolved on my tongue.

*

173

I had forgotten the almond biscuits until now. I forgot them almost immediately because the police came and some doctor who wasn't Alain, and Arlette, who went away immediately to phone Charleshall.

'I spoke to the Major,' she said when she came back.

At some point I think Alain was there. I remember him smaller, looking ill. He had probably been crying but I had never seen a man cry, might not have considered it possible. Nobody told us what had happened and I believe by then I had blanked out Julia, the river bank, Judith falling. Shock was setting in. A policeman asked questions but I replied incoherently, began to cry.

'Oh, Annie,' cried Arlette. 'There has been an accident. Madame ...' And she wiped away tears.

Where were the boys? Someone must have taken them out. Where was Julia? Sometimes there, sometimes not. She was very white. She said nothing.

That night we were put to sleep in separate rooms and in the morning I woke to find them already gone, Julia and the boys. The housekeeper told me the Major was coming, was arranging for us all to go home. I was to stay at the doctor's until sent for. Arlette had telephoned my mother. After this I lost any sense of time, except of time passing slowly, of clocks ticking, of having nothing to do, of being abandoned. Then a note came from Alain: 'Dear Annie, please keep the Monet. Forgive me for not saying goodbye.'

In the evening ... No, the next morning, the grandmother arrived and told me she was taking me home by train. She watched while I packed. She said little, only that my mother knew I was coming. As we left the room she picked up the Monet, asked, 'Is this yours?'

174

'No,' I said. 'It belongs to Dr Valences.'

'Then that's everything then,' she said.

Why the grandmother? Why by train? Where were Julia, Georgie, Tim?

'They are going to Charleshall with the Major,' I was told.

'She's dead then.' No one had told me.

'Good Heavens!'

'How is she dead?'

'What do you mean? If you're ready we must go, Annie.'

'How did she die?'

Old, weary face, hard eyes. 'She fell in the river, my dear. She drowned.' She spoke without expression. 'Now come on. And take no notice of that silly girl.'

The silly girl was Arlette, in tears. 'Oh, Annie ...'

'Come now,' said the grandmother. 'There's no need for all that.'

And a long time after, in that buffet, clink of china, buzz of conversation, smell of omelette. 'It doesn't do to dwell on what's past. It doesn't do, Annie,' and her hand over mine. A formidable little woman. She thought me rather a common child, I suspect.

'Where's Julia?' Why did I ask this?

'On her way home too. She's not very well.'

No, don't dwell on what's past, Annie.

After all, there was nothing after this except the writing of the two letters which were never answered. See, here they are. They seem to have been read more than once, at least refolded. There are creases in the paper I never put there. The creases are yellowing now, becoming fragile. My handwriting startles me, arty-crafty-schooly, large very round Os, Ts scored across boldly. I remember weeping as I wrote, but there are no obvious signs of tears so maybe a great deal of what we remember isn't true.

175

Judith was brought back and buried decently in England. My mother found this out, probably from a newspaper. I imagined the little spaniel sitting waiting on the front steps at Charleshall. I grew maudlin, nervous, I wept a great deal.

But it was all a long time ago.

I know what David will say: why not tell someone you saw Julia push her mother? The girl needed help, didn't she? Did she? Perhaps they gave her help afterwards, at the nursing home or wherever it was. Maybe she even told them. Or when shock and disbelief wore off she sobbed out what she had done on Dukie's solid bosom. Sentimental rubbish, Annie. Julia never sobbed and Dukie was no longer there.

I sit and think of her last drive with Philippe. Did they quarrel? Did she lose her head? I imagine her accelerating, taking the bend at a what-the-hell angle, going over into oblivion.

I take out the rings, the bracelet, the photograph of the schoolgirls. Then I go down to where we burn the garden rubbish and strike a match and feed the contents of Julia's box to the clean bright flames. And as I lean to blow on them gently, not wanting even a corner left, my hair catches. There is a faint crackling, the reek of burning.

In five minutes all that is left is the small pile of Julia's ashes.

'What happened to your hair?' asks David when he comes home.

'I singed it. It was in a good cause.'

I go into the studio and lock the door behind me. I put on my painting apron and pick up the palette. I feel angry. I feel angry and miserable and exhausted. I build up the colours slowly but in a kind of simmering

176

fury. The familiar oily smell rises. I pick up a clean brush and touch it to my cheek.

Then I begin.

It is finished. I lay down the brush.

The light comes from behind and above. Light fascinates me, the life it imparts, the secrets it keeps or reveals. And how to indicate the boundaries of form and substance which the eye believes it sees? How much of Julia do I see? She is on the rocking horse, waiting. She has just come in, come here, to catch her breath, to keep out of someone's way, to speak to me. 'I wish they'd all go home, Annie.' She hated other children, waiting her turn, being chosen, being left out. Usually left out. 'Julia cheats,' they said. But she didn't cheat, she simply lost interest, walked away. But is today her birthday? Have the innocuous cousins, loud, thoughtless, normal, been forced to let her play, let her share? She is in her best clothes and is uncomfortable. She has dislodged the ridiculous bow holding back one lock of hair. She has left them all outside, the shrieking children dizzy with cake and jelly and party games.

'I just want to be with you, Annie.'

She will only stay here a moment. She will be missed. Judith will come looking. Besides, she has been taught manners. But for this moment she sits, leaning forward, her arms along the horse's neck, her head on her arms. She is looking at me. She is smiling. The smile, as it rarely is, is also in her eyes.

'Hurry up, Annie.'

I hurry.

At midnight or some time after I put in the last stroke, lay down the brush.

There.

She is too tired to put on the mask, to be haughty, to

hide. There is nobody to hide from. There is nobody else here but old Carroty. Only you and me, Annie. Never ever. The flesh of her pale cheek against the flesh of her arm: how does the light fall? It falls. The guarded eyes smile. These things have risen from the deep pools of memory. In her hair the silly pink bow, pure dazzling outrageous colour. Oh, Julia, I think. But it doesn't do to weep into expensive linseed oil. It is a waste of good materials.

I do not even crawl upstairs, I sleep in the kitchen with my head on the table. Gina finds me when she comes down to make tea and toast at seven. I feel her light kiss on my hair.

'Finished?'

'Yes. I didn't say goodnight, did I?'

'I understand. Is it good?'

'Don't know.'

She looks at me, head on one side, perky little bird Gina. There are still traces of bruising about her eyes. She will never paint pictures but she may write me into a book one day.

'Cup of tea?'

She stands there while I drink as if she is protecting an invalid. She says, 'May I go and see?'

'I don't ...' I begin, but she has already gone, barefoot along the passage. I hear the door of the studio open, catch the sharp scent of oils. Silence. Then click, the door again. Feet padding. Her face is luminous.

'Ma, it's beautiful,' and then, sobering, 'sad.'

'Why is it sad?'

'I don't know.'

'But she's smiling.'

She shakes her head. She cannot explain it.

'Finished?' demands Sam, crashing in. 'Tea? Good.'

'Yes, finished.'
'Thank God.'

David is late leaving for the office. He has just learned that his street is to be redeveloped. No, the word is enhanced. It is to be enhanced with traditional cobbles and wooden bollards to keep out the traffic.

'A car-free zone,' he says.

'Cobbles are hell on the feet. It shows that planners never walk anywhere.'

I see he is wearing the tie with the red ziggurats on a purple ground. He is emotionally disturbed then.

'Look woman, just make enough cash to keep us afloat, will you? I'm thinking of retiring. I might take up astrophysics or archaeology.'

'You'll feel better later when you've drawn up a couple of wills and eaten a decent sandwich. Send Bibs out for a bottle of something.'

'She keeps a wine cellar in the blue filing cabinet.'

'But of course. I should have thought.'

'How's the portrait?'

'Go and see.'

He shrugs himself into his jacket, plods away down the passage. I stay in the kitchen doing housewifely things like piling up plates and running hot water into the sink. He is a long time coming back and when he does he stands in the doorway and says nothing, which is disconcerting.

'You must be tired,' he says at last, and then, 'You know that school photo you put up on the piano? Well, I found you in it. Grumpy-looking, with a big plait over one shoulder.'

'Julia is next to me.'

'Not the Julia in your portrait,' says David.

The boat leaks but not enough to worry intrepid

explorers. An inch in the bilge is a salutary reminder of our littleness in the face of the elements.

'Annie, we're sinking,' cries Greta. She lifts her yachty shoes up and wedges them against my rowlock.

'If you do that I can't row,' I tell her.

Gina wears a long-suffering expression, is in charge of the bailer. She thinks Greta rather silly to want to go out in the boat in a pair of pink jeans and a white strapless top. Besides, Greta has just been rude about the portrait of Julia and Gina thinks this unforgivable.

'It's too mysterious,' Greta said. 'All these shadows here and so much light over there.'

'I didn't mean to be rude about the picture,' she says now. 'I'm sure Wim will like it.'

'Perhaps.'

'Will you sell it to him?'

'No.'

No, Wim shan't have it. Julia was my friend. I loved her.

Gina grins and dips the bailer in and out like a madwoman, splashing Greta's elegant pink legs.

Lavender scent, the dry crackly grass, the breathless run down to the *bassin*.

'I don't want to swim.'

'Don't be silly. Why not? Just this once.'

This once I had persuaded her. Her hand took mine. We sank together into the cool depths.

'Annie, I'm drowning,' and the dull wet blackness of her hair spreading on the water.

'There are the boys,' I said as they flew past on their way to the river or to their den in the oaks.

'You wouldn't care if I did drown, would you?'

'How can you drown? You can swim.'

'The snakes ...'

'There aren't any snakes. You didn't really think there were, did you?'

We hang on the rim, close together. This is the first time we have been close in any way since coming here. Then she turns and floats away on her back, and I try to wring the water out of my pigtail, and above on the terrace under the mulberry Arlette bangs on a tin tray with a spoon and shouts that there is lemonade and strawberries.

We tie up the boat. Sam is putting the old deckchairs out on the lawn and is testing them gingerly with the help of a tall slender girl with fair hair.

'That must be Jenny,' says Gina.

'What happened to Hannah?'

'Oh Ma, you're ages behind. Hannah was weeks ago.'

She and Greta drift towards the chairs. I lift the oars from the boat and stand a moment on the riverbank. I remember that this morning's post brought a letter from Marion. Is she tired of Vermont? I close my eyes briefly and when I open them again I think I see a girl under the willow. She is sitting there alone. Sunlight dapples her black head. And in another garden I am running between box hedges, brushing away the ladybirds, calling and calling all the hot sultry afternoon, 'Julia. Juli ... a ... aa ...'

She seldom played the game properly but would always return with a gift, a treat: a biscuit, an apple, a piece of cake, a book. She was true in her own fashion. And all these weeks I have been running about crying 'Julia. Juli ... a ... aa ...' down the twisting paths of the past. And she has come, at last, and has brought me the painting.

I suppose one could say it was in the box.

I know it is the best I have ever done.

181

'Are you coming?' calls Gina. She and Jenny have their heads together.

Carrying the oars, I walk across the sunlit grass to join them.